Lone Star Ranger

Volume 1

A Ranger to Ride With

James J. Griffin (signature)

James J. Griffin

For Nathan
Best wishes! (signature)

For everyone, especially the young people,
who still want to read about the history of
the United States West.

1

Nathaniel Stewart had just left his house and was walking down Linden Street in his hometown of Wilmington, Delaware. In a few moments, he'd arrive at his best friend Hugh Dickinson's home. He and Hugh would meet up with a few other friends, then either head to the river for a swim, or more likely just laze around in one of the boys' back yards.

The day was pleasant for late July, the air warm with a gentle breeze blowing, not hot and sticky as it usually was this time of year. Nathaniel whistled as he walked along the tree lined street, fronted with its rows of neat brick houses with their well-kept yards and flower boxes filled with colorful blooms on the windowsills. He was fourteen years old, with unruly brown hair and eyes of the same hue. He'd recently grown a couple of inches, so had the typical thin build of most teenaged boys. He'd also recently realized that girls were beginning to interest him, and that when he walked by some of them smiled at him, then giggled for some reason. Truth be told, he had no idea *why* he was out of the blue interested in girls. All he knew was that the scrawny, dumb, silly females who'd always made pests of themselves were suddenly pretty and attractive. And one of the prettiest was Becky Palmer, with her pert turned up nose, blonde hair, and blue eyes the color of forget-me-nots. For some reason he felt he'd like to sit next to her on the front porch swing. He'd never admit that to Hugh or any of the other guys, though.

Nathaniel meandered along, not being in any particular hurry. Unexpectedly, Becky appeared at the end of the block. When she spotted Nathaniel, she waved to him and called his name.

"Nathaniel! Nathaniel Stewart!"

Nathaniel raised a hand to wave in response.

"Nathaniel! Get back to hoeing, right this minute. Those weeds aren't going to pull themselves out of the ground!"

Nathaniel was roused from his daydream by the shouting of his mother, who stood in the door of the three-room dogtrot cabin the Stewart family now occupied. The voice he'd heard calling was not Becky's, but his ma's.

"Do you hear me, Nathaniel?"

"Yes, Ma." Nathaniel sighed and lifted the hoe he'd been leaning against. He again began chopping at the tough weeds between the rows of turnips. He and his family no longer lived in their former pleasant neighborhood in Wilmington, but now on a small ranch several miles west of San Saba, Texas.

"And once you've finished weeding it will be time to milk the cow," Mrs. Stewart added.

"Can't Pa do that?" Nathaniel asked.

"He could, but he's chopping wood for me. So you need to handle that chore. Do you understand?"

"Yes, Ma." Nathaniel sighed again. How he hated Texas, and this ranch in particular! His father, Marcus, an accountant by trade, had inexplicably developed a sense of adventure and determined to join the many others heading to post-Reconstruction Texas. Within a matter of weeks, he'd bought a piece of land complete with cabin and barn, sight unseen. He'd uprooted his family, wife Adele, Nathaniel, and Nathaniel's older brother, eighteen-year-old Jonathan, and moved them all to Texas.

Nathaniel's first sight of their new home came as a shock. Instead of the tree-lined streets, neat homes, and green yards he'd grown up with in Delaware, this part of Texas was mainly flat, hot, dry, and dusty. Even the San Saba River, as it was called, was barely more than a trickle compared to the streams back home. It would hardly be a drop in the mighty Delaware River. The vegetation, what there was of it, was mostly brush, and much of it thorny. The only trees of any size grew in scattered spots along the San Saba.

Even more of an unpleasant surprise was the house; or more properly, the cabin. Back home in Wilmington, in their spacious two-story, six-room brick house, Nathaniel had his own bedroom. Here the entire family was crammed into that three room dogtrot cabin, so named because it had two sections with a covered area in the middle called a "dogtrot", since it resembled nothing so much as a chained dog's run, connecting the two. One side was a single room used as kitchen and living room, the other was divided into two small bedrooms. Nathaniel and Jonathan shared the smaller of the two rooms. Not only had Nathaniel lost his own room, he also lost his own bed. Now, he and Jonathan had to crowd into one bed— an arrangement which was cramped, to say the least. Nathaniel soon found out that Jonathan was a cover snatcher, pulling the sheets and blankets off Nathaniel and wrapping himself in them. Not that it mattered all that much once the short Texas winter and spring were over and the sweltering heat and humidity of summer set in. Covers were the last thing you needed when trying to sleep. Nathaniel and his brother wore as little as possible when crawling into bed. Actually, given their choice, both boys would have slept buck-naked, but their mother forbade any such thing. What annoyed Nathaniel was not so much Jonathan's stealing the covers as his trying to hog the whole bed. More than once, he'd been rudely awakened in the middle of the night by his brother's elbow jabbing into his ribs.

Nathaniel's friends had all been envious when they'd learned he was moving to Texas. They'd all heard tales of cattle drives, cowboys, gunfighters, and wild Indians. They were convinced Nathaniel would soon be one of their number, riding a horse, chasing cattle across the prairie, and fighting outlaws and desperadoes, downing them in a blaze of gunfire. *If only they knew the truth.* Nathaniel and his family had been in Texas for just shy of a year now, and he had yet to see any Indians at all, let alone any wild ones. The few cowboys he had seen were not handsome, riding-high-in-the-saddle men, but were usually dusty, dirty, and smelly from trailing cattle. True, they all wore guns, but he'd never seen a cowboy actually use one. As far as Nathaniel himself went, the only varmints he'd ever rounded up were the jackrabbits and rodents which were determined to eat every vegetable his mother planted.

No, the longer Nathaniel had been in Texas, the more he'd grown to despise his new life. It was dull and boring, mainly working in the daily struggle to keep the small vegetable garden him mother insisted on planting surviving. While the seventy head of long-horned cattle his father had purchased along with the ranch seemed to thrive on the tough vegetation and sparse grass, and cactus and mesquite grew in abundance, most plants wilted in the unforgiving Texas sun. Heck, Nathaniel even missed school. With their home being so far from town, the only book learning he now received was taught by his mother. The same thing went for church. Instead of going to church every Sunday, where Nathaniel could see his friends once services were over, the only clergyman the Stewarts ever saw was a circuit-riding Methodist preacher who stopped by once every few weeks. Even Reverend Pierce's long and boring sermons would be welcome right now. In fact, Nathaniel even missed his Aunt Ida, a woman he'd never looked forward to visiting. She was one of those ladies who wore far too much perfume and smothered a kid with unwanted kisses. Right now, he'd welcome some of those kisses, perfume and all. Isolated here in the middle of nowhere, he missed having companions to pal around with. And he'd certainly never meet a girl like Becky Palmer way out here.

As the afternoon wore on, Nathaniel kept hoeing half-heartedly at the weeds choking the garden. He looked up at the sound of an approaching horse and rider.

"Howdy, little brother," Jonathan shouted as he rode up and dismounted. "You keepin' the weeds from takin' over the place?"

8

"I'm doin' my best."

"Well, you keep at it." Jonathan pulled Nathaniel's straw hat off his head, tousled his brother's hair and laughed. "Wrangle those pests right outta the ground. I've gotta take care of my horse."

"He's gotta take care of his horse," Nathaniel muttered under his breath once Jonathan headed for the barn. He felt a twinge of jealousy. Unlike Nathaniel, his brother had taken to Texas life like a merganser took to water in the Delaware Bay. Jonathan had easily learned to rope and ride and was on his way to becoming a top hand. He had bought a horse, a sorrel gelding he named Big Red, and sat in the saddle as if he'd been born there. He'd laughed himself silly when he came home with the horse and Nathaniel asked if a gelding was a boy or girl horse. He'd also bought a six-gun, one of the new and still rare Smith and Wesson American cartridge pistols. He'd explained to Nathaniel a cartridge gun was a lot more efficient than the old-fashioned cap and ball pistols, such as the Navy Colt, that most men still carried. It didn't take long for Jonathan to become a crack shot with that pistol, as well as the Winchester rifle he bought. Jonathan had a natural ability with firearms. Besides taking charge of the Stewarts' herd, he also found work on a neighboring ranch, helping with branding and doctoring their cattle.

Nathaniel finally gave up on yanking more weeds out of the hard, sun-baked ground. He went into the barn, got a bucket and the milking stool, and started for the small pen which held the milk cow. By the time he finished milking Bess, Jonathan had groomed, fed, and watered Big Red, along with Buck, the plow and wagon horse. He tossed some hay to the cow.

"Figured I'd save you a bit of work, Nathaniel," he said.

"I appreciate that, big brother. Man, I'm sure sick of weedin' that garden. Nothin' grows good in it anyway."

"Don't let Ma hear you say that. She's determined to have a garden just like back in Delaware."

"Wish we *were* back in Delaware."

9

"You just gotta learn to be a cowboy like me, that's all." Jonathan gave Nathaniel a playful backhanded slap to his stomach. Nathaniel responded with a shove to his brother's ribs.

"You just asked for it," Jonathan said, with a grin. "And you're sure gonna get it." He shoved Nathaniel in the chest, pushing him to the ground.

Jonathan being four years older was more heavily muscled, but Nathaniel was quicker. When Jonathan dove at him, Nathaniel easily rolled out of the way. Jonathan hit the ground with a thud. Before he could recover, Nathaniel jumped on his back, pinning him. The stronger Jonathan tossed Nathaniel off, then wrapped his arms around him. The brothers rolled over and over, raising a cloud of dust as they struggled.

Marcus stepped out of the cabin.

"Jonathan! Nathaniel! Both of you stop that fighting, right now!" When the boys failed to respond, he grabbed a pail of old dishwater from where it sat next to the door, walked up to the brothers, and dumped it over them.

"Pa! What'd you do that for?" Jonathan exclaimed. He and Nathaniel rolled onto their backs, chests heaving as they gasped for breath.

"You two weren't listening. How many times have your mother and I told you not to fight?"

"We were just havin' some fun, Pa," Nathaniel answered.

"That's right. We were just wrestlin' is all," Jonathan added.

"Well, you can burn off some of that energy by cutting some more firewood after supper. Your mother's certainly not going to be happy I used the water for her garden to stop you two," Marcus said. "Meantime, our meal's just about on the table. You both wash up and get inside."

"All right, Pa," Jonathan said. He and Nathaniel pulled themselves to their feet and headed for the pump and wash bench behind the cabin.

Cleaning up was another thing Nathaniel despised about his new home. Back in Delaware, he had a wash stand, pitcher, and basin in his room. It was a simple matter to heat water on the

10

kitchen stove and carry some upstairs for bathing. The house even had a bathtub in a separate room off the back. Here in Texas, with water scarce, the entire family used water sparingly from the pump to fill a shallow trough, then wash up as best they could. Towels, soap, and washcloths were on the bench next to the pump. A full bath involved dragging a zinc tub from the dogtrot into the kitchen, then heating kettles of water. Filling and then emptying the tub was a major chore, so a hot bath was a rare treat indeed. More often, the boys would bathe in Wallace Creek, which ran along the back boundary of the ranch.

Nathaniel and Jonathan pulled off their hats and neckerchiefs, then peeled out of their sweat-soaked shirts. Nathaniel pumped the trough full, then both ducked their heads into the refreshing water. They turned at the sound of fast-approaching horses.

"That looks like trouble," Jonathan said. Close to a dozen men were riding for the house at a gallop. All had rifles or pistols in their hands. Jonathan pulled his Smith and Wesson from the holster on his right hip. Marcus had also heard the men's approach. He came into the dogtrot holding an over and under shotgun.

"What do you men want?" he called.

The foremost rider leveled his rifle and fired once, his bullet knocking Marcus off his feet. He hit the cabin wall and slid to the ground. The shotgun blasted its load of buckshot harmlessly into the dogtrot roof when Marcus' finger tightened on its triggers as he died.

"Get down," Jonathan shouted. He pushed Nathaniel aside, then fired a snap shot at one of the raiders. The bullet took the man in his stomach. He grunted, grabbed his middle and slumped over his horse's neck, then tumbled to the dirt.

Two of the men returned Jonathan's fire. Blood blossomed on his chest when their bullets tore into him. He staggered and fell to his face. Nathaniel lunged from where his brother had pushed him behind the trough, wrested the pistol from Jonathan's hand, rolled over twice, and shot. His bullet struck one of the men in the left arm, then an impact like a sledgehammer's blow hit Nathaniel's head. The last thing he remembered before falling into a sea of whirling black was his mother, calling his name.

2

Texas Ranger Lieutenant Robert Berkeley ordered the column of seven men he led to a halt atop a low rise which overlooked the San Saba River. The river had cut a small valley through this mostly flat or gently rolling part of Texas. Gazing at the horizon, he spoke to the man next to him. He pointed to a column of thick black smoke rising into the otherwise clear blue sky.

"I don't like the looks of that smoke over yonder. What do you think, Jeb?"

Ranger Jeb Rollins thumbed back his Stetson and ran a hand across his sweaty forehead.

"Don't like the looks of it either, Bob. It's way too much smoke for a campfire. But it's not enough to be a prairie fire, less'n it just got started. I reckon it's someone's house or barn blazin'."

"You recollect any ranches down that way?"

Jeb thought for a minute.

"Only one near that spot is the old Stillwell place, about six miles from here. Lies along Wallace Creek as I recall. It was abandoned for quite a spell, but I heard some Easterners name of Stewart bought the spread and moved in there some months back. You think the men we've been trailin' might have hit the place? Those folks wouldn't stand a chance if they did."

"I wouldn't bet my hat against it," Bob answered. "We'd better get over there and find out. Men, let's ride!" He dug his spurs into his horse's sides. Alongside him Jeb did the same,

13

spurring his paint into motion. Their horses broke into a fast lope, the rest of the Rangers strung out behind them. They maintained that pace for a good four miles then as they neared the old Stillwell ranch, with a thin haze of smoke now drifting on the breeze, urged them into a gallop. Once they were within a half mile of the place, the smoke now thicker and making their eyes water, they pushed their mounts into a dead run. As they neared the ranch they pulled rifles from their scabbards or pistols from their holsters. If those renegades were still looting the place, they were about to receive a rude surprise. The Rangers would ride in without warning, guns blazing, and ask questions once the smoke had settled.

There was a thick screen of scrub brush surrounding the Stewart ranch. The Rangers burst through that but quickly pulled their horses to a halt, realizing they were too late to help anyone. The cabin and barn had both collapsed and were now little more than heaps of still-burning timbers. Three bodies lay sprawled on the ground, a man and a woman near the burning cabin, another man further out. A pair of boots could be seen protruding from where the dogtrot's roof had evidently fallen on another body when it caved in.

"Kelly, Morton, you two check the area around here. Make sure those renegades haven't holed up nearby. Don't want them jumpin' us," Berkeley ordered. "The rest of you, let's do what we can for these folks. Harrison, Jennings, try'n pull what's left of the poor hombre under that roof outta there before the flames get to him."

"Don't think it'll make much difference to him, Bob," Ed Jennings answered.

"I know it won't, but it wouldn't be right to let him burn up if we can give him a decent burial instead. "

"All right."

The men Bob had sent to look for the outlaws headed back into the brush, while the others dismounted. Bob and Jeb first went to the woman. She was clearly dead, having been shot several times. Bob muttered a curse.

"Men who'd shoot down a woman like that are the worst scum I can imagine, Bob," Jeb said. "They deserve to be killed like the rabid skunks they are."

"They will be, soon as we catch up to 'em," Bob answered. "We've been gainin' on 'em steady. It won't be too long now until we get 'em in our gunsights. And when we do..."

One of the other Rangers called from where he had rolled a young man onto his back.

"This one's done for too, Bob," he called. "Took a couple of slugs in his chest. Young kid, too. Couldn't have been more'n eighteen or nineteen years old. Real shame."

For several weeks now, he and his men had been chasing the gang of outlaws which had apparently attacked and murdered this family. Every time they came close to capturing them, somehow they managed to slip away. The leader of the bunch was obviously a clever individual who knew the territory well. He seemed to know every escape route for miles around.

"This man's still alive," another Ranger called. He was hunkered alongside the man Jonathan had shot. "Dunno for how long, though. He's gut-shot, got plugged plumb in the center of his belly. I figure he's one of the men we've been after."

Bob and Jeb hurried over to the dying outlaw. Bob looked down at the mortally wounded man. He had long black hair, and whiskers stubbled his face and neck. Dust coating his clothes indicated he had been riding long and hard.

"Texas Rangers, mister," Bob said. "Looks like you don't have much time left. Who were you ridin' with, and where's your outfit hole up?"

The wounded outlaw groaned, then shook his head.

"I ain't gonna tell you nothin', Ranger," he muttered.

"Listen to me," Bob urged. "You've been part of a bunch that's been killin' and robbin' folks all over this part of Texas. You've even killed a woman and a young kid here. You might want to make peace with your Maker before you cash in your chips."

"I didn't kill that woman or kid. Caught a slug before I could even get off a shot. Far as makin' peace with God, I reckon it's too late for that. Besides, I've been headed to meet the Devil since the day I was born. My pappy kept tellin' me that. Looks like I made certain he was gonna be right. And I sure ain't gonna give up my pards to any lawman."

"They weren't worried about you," Jeb said. "Seems to me they left you here to die, rather'n tryin' to find a doc and get you some help. Dunno about you, but I sure wouldn't protect anyone who left me alone with a bullet in my guts."

"Just my bad luck, is all," the man replied. "Knew I'd catch a slug, sooner or later." He coughed, and blood trickled from the corner of his mouth. His breathing was becoming more shallow and ragged.

"You mind at least givin' us your name, mister?" Bob asked.

"What difference does it make what my name is?"

"We can let your kinfolks know what happened to you."

The outlaw gave a weak laugh.

"Sure. Tell 'em their boy died an outlaw. That'd make 'em real happy. Besides, I've got no kin left."

"Mister, you don't have long, probably only a few minutes," Jeb said. "Why not do one thing right in your life and tell us where to find your pardners? Help us stop 'em from killin' anyone else."

"Not gonna do that. But I reckon it won't hurt to tell you my name. It's Lance. Lance Ches..."

The outlaw shuddered, sighed, and breathed his last.

"He's gone, Bob," Jeb said. "Took whatever he knew with him, even his full name."

"Don't matter. We'll catch up to those men, and real soon. Meantime, let's try'n see if we can salvage anything out of what's left of this place. These folks might have some kin we can track down and get whatever possessions we can find to 'em. They'd appreciate that. And maybe we'll come up with some grub those outlaws might've missed. Almost feels like we're stealin' from the dead ourselves, but it'd be a shame to let any supplies we can use go to waste."

"All right, Bob."

Hoot Harrison and Ed Jennings had pulled the older man's body free of the burning cabin. The Easterner was still clutching his shotgun. They moved him away from the flames, then rejoined Berkeley and Rollins.

"That man was dead before the roof fell on him," Hoot explained. "He took a bullet square in the center of his chest. Got off both barrels of his shotgun before he died, though. I doubt he managed to hit any of those renegades."

Jim Kelly and Dan Morton returned from scouting the area surrounding the ranch.

"Those hombres didn't stick around, Bob," Jim reported. "Must've driven the stock off from this ranch. Tracks of a whole passel of cattle headed southeast, and bein' driven hard. We could probably catch up with 'em without too much trouble. Couldn't be more'n an hour or two since they hit."

Bob looked at the lowering sun, which was nearing the western horizon. Clouds were also building to the northwest. He shook his head.

"Much as I'd like to try, we'd never find 'em before dark. It's a new moon tonight, plus it looks like it might rain a bit, so even trailin' a herd of cattle would be real tough. We'll spend the night here, bury these folks, then go after those renegades right after sunup. They're probably not gonna drive that herd all night, and even if they do, they can't keep pushin' 'em too hard. We should find 'em without too much trouble. Meantime, help the rest of the boys try'n douse those fires and see if there's anything we can save. Looks to me like the wind's gonna pick up soon, and we don't need any embers blowin' around and startin' a wildfire. I don't think there's enough rain in those clouds to stop one if it gets a good start. Once the fires are out cover the bodies so the scavengers can't get at 'em."

"All right, Bob."

Jim and Dan dismounted and joined two of the men who were pulling buckets of water from the well and tossing them on the barn, while Bob and Jeb headed for what was left of the cabin. They began poking through the still smoldering ruins.

"Looks like they made sure nothing was left," Bob said.

"Sure seems that way," Jeb agreed. His gaze settled on a plank door set into the ground at an angle. It was partially covered by a section of the cabin's back wall which had fallen on it.

"That looks like a root cellar. Reckon I'll check and see if there's any vegetables in there, or maybe even some preserves the missus put up. Anything at all would be a nice change from bacon and beans."

Jeb walked over to the door, kicked aside the smoldering section of wall, and lifted the door. When he did, a young boy charged out of the cellar. He ran straight into Jeb, burying his head in the Ranger's stomach, driving the air out of his lungs and knocking him to the ground. He dove on top of Jeb, swinging his fists wildly.

"You killed my brother!" he screamed. One of his punches connected with the side of Jeb's jaw. Jeb grabbed the youngster's wrists. The boy continued to struggle.

"Hold still, kid. Get offa me. None of us killed your brother. We're Texas Rangers. Hold still, I said," Jeb repeated, when the boy continued to resist. "I don't want to hurt you. Just get offa me and we'll get this all straightened out."

Bob and Jim hurried over to help their fellow Ranger. They grabbed Nathaniel's shoulders and lifted him gently from atop Jeb.

"Take it easy, son," Bob said. "Like Jeb says, we're not gonna hurt you. We're not part of the outfit that killed your folks. We're Texas Rangers. Been on the trail of those murderers for quite a spell now. Just wish we could've caught up with 'em sooner, so we might've been able to save your kin. We're gonna let go of you now. All right?"

Nathaniel nodded his head, sniffling. He was trying desperately not to cry.

"Let him go, Jim."

Nathaniel's arms were released. Jeb came to his feet and

18

stood rubbing the lump rising on his jaw.

"You pack quite a wallop there, kid," he said.

"I'm sorry, mister," Nathaniel answered. "It's just that I thought... I thought..." His voice trailed off.

"We understand, son," Bob said.

Jim looked at the gash across Nathaniel's scalp. The boy's hair was matted down with sweat and dried blood.

"Bob, this boy's hurt," he said. "Appears to me he's been shot. Looks like he was mighty lucky and the bullet just creased him. Reckon I'd better patch him up and make sure, though."

"All right, Jim," Bob agreed. "We'll take him over to that cottonwood. He needs to get out of the sun before he gets a bad burn, bein' shirtless like he is. I know the sun's settin', but it's still high enough to roast a man's skin."

"You go with the lieutenant, son," Jim said. "I'll be right back. I'll fetch some water for the boy, too." He headed for his horse, to retrieve the rudimentary medical kit he carried in his saddlebags. Bob and Jeb led Nathaniel to the scant shade of a half-dead cottonwood. The tree had taken root well away from any good source of water, but had somehow survived for quite a few years. However, it was now losing its struggle to live.

"Sit down and lean against the tree, son," Bob ordered. "What's your name?"

"It's Nathaniel. Nathaniel Stewart."

"That your ma and pa got killed over yonder?"

"Yeah. Yeah. And Jonathan, my big brother. Those men killed... killed..."

"You don't need to say anything more... Nathaniel. We know what happened."

"You the one who gut-shot that son of a—um—sidewinder, Nate?" Jeb asked, careful not to use the term he really wanted to use to describe the dead outlaw.

"My name's Nathaniel."

Jeb shook his head. He smiled, trying to reassure the boy he was safe, and with friends.

"That's too much of a mouthful. Long as you don't mind, I

reckon we'll call you Nate."

"I guess it'll be all right," Nathaniel said, with a shrug.

"Fine. Now, did you shoot that hombre?"

"Hombre?" Nathaniel was puzzled.

"Spanish for man," Bob explained. "You'll hear a lot of that mixed in with English here in Texas."

"Oh. No, no I didn't shoot him. My brother did that... just before he got shot himself."

"I see."

"But I think I did shoot one," Nathaniel said. "I took my brother's gun from his hand and pulled the trigger. Saw one of the other men grab his arm and heard him yelp. Then, I guess I got shot, because I don't remember anything after that."

"Nate, this is important," Jeb said. "Which arm?"

"The left."

"Good. Once we catch up to that bunch it'll help identify him."

Jim returned, carrying his medical kit and a canteen. The rest of the Rangers were with him.

"Y'all can stop questionin' this poor boy until I fix him up," he said, in a west Texas twang. "You keep jawin' at him like that and he's liable to keel right over on us."

"All right, Jim," Bob said. To Nathaniel he added, "Jim here's kind of the troop doctor. He had some medical trainin' while fightin' for the Confederacy. He's as good at fixin' broken bones, stitchin' up cuts or knife wounds, and diggin' bullets out of a man as any doctor I've ever met."

"And I drink a whole sight less than a lot of those," Jim added. "Now let me take a look at you, son. What's your name?"

"It's Nathaniel... Nate."

"All right, Nate. I'm gonna take a looksee at this head of yours, then patch you up. You're gonna be just fine. Take a drink before I get started."

He opened his canteen and handed it to Nathaniel. Nathaniel took it and drank greedily.

"Not too much," Jim cautioned. "Don't want you gettin' a

bellyache from drinkin' too much. Course, it won't be as bad a bellyache as the one your brother gave that hombre lyin' over there. Lead bellyaches are the worst kind. Reckon your brother must've been a man to ride the river with. I'd wager he'd have made a fine Ranger." He grinned. Nathaniel managed a thin smile of his own.

"There, that's better," Jim said. He parted Nathaniel's hair to examine the bullet slash across his scalp. He poured some water from his canteen onto a scrap of cloth and used that to wash away dirt, dried blood, and bits of flesh.

"I hate to do this to you, Nate, but you're gonna need a few stitches to pull your skin back together so it can heal. You're a real lucky kid. Fraction of an inch lower and you'd be dead."

"That means he must have an even thicker skull than you, Jim," Jeb said, chuckling.

"See if I take the bullet out of your hide next time you catch a slug, Jeb," Jim retorted. "Nate, this is gonna hurt somethin' fierce. You think you'll be able to handle it?"

Nathaniel swallowed hard. "Do I have a choice?"

"I'm afraid not, son."

"Then I'll have to."

"Good. You're a brave lad. I reckon you'd do to ride the river with, too."

Jim took a razor from his bag, along with a scalpel, thick needle and thread, and a small flask of whiskey. "This whiskey is strictly for medicinal purposes, Nate. I use it to clean and sterilize my instruments." He doused the bullet crease with some of the whiskey, poured some more over the razor, then shaved off a strip of Nathaniel's hair from around the wound. Nathaniel flinched.

"You're gonna scalp me like those wild Indians I've heard about," he protested.

"No, I'm not, Nate. I promise you that. You do need to keep still while I'm workin' on you, though. I know it's not easy, but try'n not move as best you can, so I don't accidentally take off another chunk of your scalp. All right?"

"All right, sir."

"Sir? Who's 'sir'? My name's Jim. Don't you forget it, you hear?"

"Yessir, sir... I mean, Jim."

"That's better. I'll get through this quick as I can. Here, take this bandanna. There's a knot in it. Put it in your mouth. If the pain gets to be too much, bite down on it, hard as you can. That'll help some."

Nathaniel took the piece of cloth and did as told. He clamped his teeth down hard. Jim picked up his scalpel, doused it with whiskey, then the wound again. He used the scalpel to trim the slash's ragged edges. Nathaniel bit down so hard on the cloth he was certain his jaw would bust or his teeth would shatter. His eyes watered with the pain.

"You're doin' just fine, Nate," Jim assured him. "That was the worst of it." He picked up the needle and thread, soaked them with whiskey, and efficiently sewed up the wound. Once done, he coated it thickly with salve, placed a clean strip of cloth over it, and tied another strip of cloth over that and around Nathaniel's head to hold it in place.

"I'm all done, Nate," Jim said. "You can let go of the bandanna now. That wasn't all that bad, was it?"

Nathaniel pulled the cloth from his mouth.

"No, not too bad," he half-whispered.

"You don't need to lie, Nate," Jeb said. "I know that hurt like the devil. But you took it like a grown man, son. You can be proud of yourself."

"Thanks, sir," Nathaniel said.

"Whoa. Enough of that 'sir' stuff. Like Jim said, none of us in this outfit are named sir. My name's Jeb. Reckon I'd better introduce you to the rest of the boys. This here's Lieutenant Robert Berkeley, although everyone generally calls him Bob. We're pretty informal in the Rangers, not like the Army. Next to him's Henry Harrison, better known as Hoot. Alongside him's Ed Jennings, then we have Dan Morton, and finally those two ugly look-alike hombres are Tom and Tim Tomlinson. We branded

Tim with that scar on his cheek so we can tell which is which. Boys, any of you didn't catch his name this here's Nathaniel Stewart... only we're gonna call him Nate."

"Don't listen to one word this ring-tailed liar says," Tim said. "Jeb's always tellin' whoppers. I got this scar from a Comanche's arrow."

Tim and his brother were identical twins, with blonde hair and blue eyes.

"Don't believe my brother, either," Tom said. "He gave himself that scar when his razor slipped while he was shavin'."

"Way I heard it, a *senorita* at Rosa's Cantina in El Paso give it to you, Tim," Hoot said, laughing.

"That's enough out of all of you," Bob ordered. "Start settin' up camp. Nate," he continued. "Before we realized there was anyone left alive we decided to spend the night here, then start after those renegades first thing in the morning. It's almost dusk, so it'll be too late to keep after 'em tonight. Since we've found you still in one piece, I reckon I need to ask your permission to use your place."

"Sure," Nathaniel agreed. "I guess it'll be okay, but shouldn't you ask..." He stopped short, his voice cracking and his eyes filling with tears.

The lieutenant put a comforting hand on Nathaniel's shoulder.

"It's all right, Nate. Go ahead and cry if you need to. Won't be any of us here think any less of you. We've all lost loved ones or friends. Unless you'd like things done different, we'd planned on buryin' your folks at sunup."

Nathaniel sniffled and ran an arm under his nose.

"No. I think I'm all right," he said. "And I know my pa'd sure like to stay right here. I guess my ma and Jonathan would like that too. We'll... we'll bury them here, on the ranch."

"Good. Mind if I ask you another question?"

"What's that?"

"The reason Jeb opened that root cellar is to find any food which might be in there that we could use. We've been on the trail for weeks now, and bacon, beans, and biscuits every day sure gets tiresome. We were hopin' to find some vegetables or maybe even some preserves your ma might've put up. Is it all right if we still do that? I'd imagine you're gettin' mighty hungry yourself."

"Sure, sure, that'd be okay."

"We're much obliged. Tim, you and Tom round up any grub you can find. Tim, you'll be cook tonight. I reckon we'd better set up a guard overnight, just in case those renegades send a couple of men back to see if they missed anything. I'll set the watches after supper. Nate, what happened to your shirt? You're gonna need it."

"My brother and I were washin' up for supper when those men attacked us. I think it must've burned up with the cabin. Might still be by the wash bench, though."

"Good. Hoot, you see if you can rustle up Nate's shirt. If not, get him your spare. It'll be a mite too big for him, but you're the closest to his size."

"Right away, Bob."

"Dan, Ed, take care of the dead. Make sure you cover 'em good so the scavengers can't get at 'em."

"Um, Bob?" Morton said.

"Yeah, Dan?"

"What about the dead outlaw? Doesn't seem fittin' he should be planted here with the folks he helped murder."

"You're right," Bob agreed. "Take him off somewhere and dig a shallow grave for him, or leave him for the buzzards and coyotes. Far as I'm concerned, that's all he deserves. Jim, get the horses settled. Nate, if you feel you're up to it, I'd like to ask you a few questions. That'll help us when we catch up to the men who did this."

"I'll try to answer them, if I can," Nathaniel said.

"Good. Jeb, you stay here with me. The rest of you, get busy."

While the other Rangers went about setting up camp for the night, Bob and Jeb questioned Nathaniel about the attack on the Stewart ranch earlier that day.

"Nate, just tell me as best you can what exactly happened," Bob requested.

"Sure," Nate answered. "Like I said before, Jonathan and I were just washin' up for supper. We heard a bunch of men ridin' real fast. Jonathan spotted 'em first and pulled out his gun. My dad must've heard 'em too, because he came outside holdin' his shotgun. They killed him, first thing. Then Jonathan pushed me behind the trough. He shot one of the outlaws, then he got shot. I knew he was dead, the way he fell. So I crawled over to him, got his gun, and managed to get off a shot. Didn't knock anyone off his horse like Jonathan did, though. I'm not much good with a gun or horse. Jonathan certainly was. He loved bein' a cowboy."

"I'm sure he did," Bob said. "Nate, do you recollect how you got in the root cellar?"

"No, I surely don't." Nathaniel shook his head. "All I remember is firin' Jonathan's gun, then everything went black. I guess I must have come to, then crawled into the cellar. I figure I was lucky those men didn't see I was still alive."

"You sure were, son," Jeb agreed. "Dang lucky. Nate, we didn't find any six-gun near you, nor your brother. My guess is one of those hombres must've picked up the gun while you were still unconscious. Can you tell us how many there were?"

"I'm not sure. Nine or ten, maybe a couple more."

"Can you tell us what any of them looked like?" Bob asked.

Again, Nathaniel shook his head. "I wish I could, but I can't. Everything happened so fast."

"It's all right," Bob reassured him.

"Nate, you don't happen to know what kind of pistol your brother wore, do you?" Jeb asked.

"I sure do. It was a Smith and Wesson American cartridge revolver. Jonathan was real proud of that gun. He even had his initials carved into the handle. He liked to talk about how much better his cartridge gun was than the old-fashioned cap and ball Colts."

Bob and Jeb exchanged glances. Jeb whistled.

"That's a mighty rare gun in these parts," he said. "If we find the man carryin' that Smith and Wesson, it's more'n likely he'll be one of the men who killed your folks."

"What about any horses?" Bob continued. "We didn't find any around the place, so those raiders must've stolen them along with the cattle. What's your horse look like?"

"I didn't have one," Nathaniel said. "Never much liked horses. My brother had one, though. A sorrel he called Big Red. Red had a star on his forehead and one white foot."

"Which foot?"

"The left front."

"So if we find your brother's horse that will also help identify the raiders," Bob said. "What about brands? What was your dad's brand?"

"My dad wouldn't brand his cattle," Nathaniel said. "He thought it was cruel. Jonathan's horse wasn't branded either. Neither was Buck, our plow horse."

"Just like Sam Maverick," Jeb said. "Well, there goes any chance of provin' the stolen cattle came from this place. Bob, I reckon it's time we let Nate try'n get a little rest. He might want some time with his folks, too."

"That's a good idea, Jeb. You go with him. Nate, it's not gonna be easy for you, but you should probably take Jeb's suggestion. Take as much time as you need with your family. Say some prayers for 'em and tell 'em you love 'em. Cry over 'em if you need to. There's no shame in that. Jeb'll stay with you long as you need. By the time you're set, supper should be ready. We need to get settled what you're gonna do next. We can talk about that while we eat."

Jeb put his arm around Nathaniel's shoulders.

"C'mon, Nate. It's time you said goodbye to your folks."

He took Nathaniel to where his parents and brother lay side by side, covered with blankets.

"Nate, you want me to stay with you, or would you rather be by yourself for a few minutes?"

"I think I'd like the company," Nate said. His voice quivered and his chin trembled as he struggled to keep him emotions in check.

"All right. I'll be here long as you need. Do you want to see their faces again, or just remember 'em the way you last saw 'em?"

"I... I don't rightly know."

Tears began streaming down Nathaniel's cheeks, and he broke into sobs. He stood crying for a few moments, then uncovered his mother, father and brother. Luckily, none of their faces bore any wounds. They looked peaceful in death.

"Jonathan," Nathaniel said. "I'm sure gonna miss you, big brother. I guess you'll never get the chance to teach me how to cowboy. Maybe that's for the best. I'd probably just have made a fool of myself, or fallen off Big Red and broken my neck. I don't have the knack for cowboyin' that you did."

A sob wracked his body before he could continue.

"Pa, I know making a go of it in Texas was your dream. If you can hear me, even though you might not believe this, I wanted it to come true for you. Yeah, I wanted to go back home, but I sure would never have left you and Ma. I hope God has a ranch for you up in Heaven."

"Ma, I love you so much. I don't know what else to say, except that I'll always try and make you proud of me. You're the best mother anyone could ask for. I wish I could've done something to stop you from dying. There's some Texas Rangers here who are after the men who did this. Once they catch them, they'll take care of them. They promised me that. Guess there's not much else to say, except I'll pray to God for you every day, that you're all with Him."

Nathaniel knelt alongside his mother and father and bent down to kiss them goodbye, then tousled Jonathan's hair one last time. He pulled the blankets back over their faces.

"I'm ready, Jeb."

His head bent in sorrow, Nathaniel started back for where the Rangers were gathering for supper, with Jeb at his side.

They had gone perhaps a hundred feet when Nathaniel turned back to gaze at the bodies of his parents and brother. The sorrow in his eyes now changed to a look of anger.

"Pa, Ma, Jonathan," he shouted. "I'm goin' to make sure those men pay for what they did to you. I don't know when, or how, but no matter how long it takes, I'll make them pay."

"Now's not the time to worry about that, son," Jeb said. "Right now, you need food and sleep. Let's go eat."

Out of respect for Nathaniel, supper was a mostly silent affair, without the usual joking and kidding that ordinarily was part of the evening meal, a way for the hard-riding Rangers, who faced danger and death almost every day, to release tension and let off steam. Instead of the ordinary meal of beans, bacon, and biscuits, there were thick beefsteaks. Nathaniel, despite his loss, was hungrier than he realized, and downed a plateful of steak, beans, and half a dozen biscuits. However, he winced at his first taste of the strong black coffee the Rangers drank. It was a much more bitter brew than what his mother had made.

"Coffee a little strong for you, Nate?" Bob asked.

"No. No, not at all," Nathaniel said, still choking. "Just a bit more bite to it than what my ma made."

"Coffee like this keeps a man goin'," Dan said. "That, and good grub. Tim, you did a fine job cookin' up these steaks. Sure were a welcome change from bacon. You put that cow to good use."

"Quiet, Dan," Bob warned. "Watch your tongue."

Nathaniel had stabbed another piece of meat with his fork. He stopped with it halfway to his mouth and looked at it.

"Where... where'd you get this meat?"

"Just some ol' cow me'n Tom found lyin' dead in the scrub," Tim said.

Nathaniel looked at the burned remains of the cowshed and enclosure which had held Bess, the milk cow. She was nowhere in sight.

"Tell me the truth, Tim. This here meat's from Bess, our cow, ain't it? Ain't it?"

"Yeah, I reckon it is," Tim answered, not quite able to meet Nathaniel's gaze. "Sorry, Nate."

"Nate, those raiders killed your cow," Jeb tried to explain. "We hardly ever see fresh meat, unless one of us downs a pronghorn or mebbe a javelina, so it just didn't seem right to let that meat go to waste. If we hadn't taken it, the coyotes and buzzards would have ripped her apart, then whatever they left the flies would have gone after. At least this way your cow filled the bellies of some mighty tired and hungry men, rather than the scavengers. Try'n understand, son."

Nathaniel dropped his plate to the dirt.

"I'm not hungry, all of a sudden. I guess I'll try and get some sleep now."

He went over to where the Rangers had made him a bed out of their spare blankets, pulled off his boots, and slid under the covers. His soft sobs drifted on the night air.

"I'm sorry, fellers," Dan said. "Didn't mean to upset the boy like that."

"It's not your fault, Dan," Bob assured him. "He would've figured it out sooner or later anyway. He's had a big loss today, and this is just one more thing that's gone from his life. Right now, cryin' to get the hurt out of him's probably the best thing for him. That, and sleep. Speaking of which, we've got a lot of hard ridin' ahead of us tomorrow. It's time we turn in. Dan, you and Ed take the first watch. Jim and Hoot will relieve you. Jeb and I will take third. Tim and Tom, you'll have the last watch. Now, let's clean up and get to bed."

3

The Rangers wanted to resume their pursuit of the outlaws as soon as possible, but first they had to attend to the somber task of burying Nathaniel's parents and brother, so Bob roused them an hour before sunrise. He let Nathaniel sleep a bit later than his men.

"Nate, time to get up," he said, gently shaking the boy's shoulders. "We've got a long day ahead of us."

"Huh?" Nathaniel lay there for a moment, confused, then the memories of the day previous came flooding back. He sat up, blearily, and rubbed sleep from his eyes.

"How'd you sleep, son? And how's your head?"

"All right, I guess. My head's still sore, but doesn't hurt all that bad." Despite everything that had happened, exhaustion had finally overtaken Nathaniel, so he slept soundly once he drifted off.

"Good. Breakfast'll be ready soon. By the time we eat, the sun'll be just comin' up. We'll bury your folks then. Meantime, take care of what needs doin'. Tom's got a bucket of water for washin' up."

Nathaniel tossed back the blankets and stood up, looking around in confusion for a moment. He knew what the lieutenant meant by taking care of what needed doin', but where to do it? The outhouse had burned along with the rest of the buildings. He decided on a large clump of four-foot-high prickly pear a few yards off. He headed behind that, relieved himself, then joined the Rangers, who were already gathered around a fire, eating.

They greeted him warmly, their eyes friendly. All of those men had lost friends or loved ones to outlaws, so they understood exactly what Nathaniel was going through. He splashed water from the bucket on his face and neck, then Tom handed him a tin plate containing biscuits and beans, and a tin mug of coffee.

"It ain't the fanciest grub, Nate, but it's tasty, and it'll stick to your ribs."

"Thanks, Tom." Nathaniel took a fork and knife, then began digging into his food.

"Nate, we have to decide what to do with you," Bob said while they ate. "You can't stay here by yourself, that's for certain. Do you have any kin who might take you in?"

"I've got an aunt and uncle back in Delaware, but I don't know about livin' with 'em."

"Why not?"

"They've got eight kids of their own. Takin' in another mouth to feed would be mighty hard on 'em. Besides, my Aunt Ida's all right, but my Uncle Henry don't like me all that much. Me'n him don't see eye to eye."

"I see. And you have no relatives in Texas."

"No. My pa decided to move down here. My folks and Jonathan were my only family, besides Aunt Ida and Uncle Henry."

"How about any friends? Do you think there's someone in San Saba you could stay with, at least until you decide for certain what you want to do?"

"No, not anyone. We didn't get into town all that often. I don't know anybody there, except maybe to say hello."

"Nate, I hate to keep askin' these questions, but they are important," Bob said. "Did your father have any money about the place, or perhaps in the San Saba bank?"

"He had an account at the bank, now that you mention it. I'm not sure how much money was left, though. I think he took a lot of it to spend fixin' up the ranch."

Bob sighed.

"Well, we have a real problem here. Nate, we have to get back on the trail of those renegades. You surely can't come with us."

"Why not, Bob?" Hoot asked.

"Well, for one thing, Nate's too young. He's also admitted he's not much of a rider. He wouldn't be able to keep up with us. For that matter, he's got no horse. Nate, I think the best thing for you to do would be go into San Saba and see if your dad had any money left in the bank. If he did, it's yours now. Take that out, buy some new clothes, then use the rest to get home to Delaware. I also think you should have a doctor check that head wound. Jim's real good, as far as it goes, but you really need to have a real physician check you over."

"But I don't want to leave my folks behind," Nathaniel answered. His eyes welled with tears.

"I know you don't, son. But think this through. You've got no living family here and no friends. Where would you live? What would you do for money? At least back in Delaware you have an aunt who will take care of you. And perhaps you can patch things up with your uncle. I don't see where there's a choice here. Jeb."

"Yeah, Bob?"

"You've got some leave coming. I want you to take that. You'll bring Nate to San Saba. Find him a doctor first off, then see to what else needs tending. Stay with him until his affairs are settled and he's on a stage heading back north, to get a train back home. You needn't worry about catching up with us once Nate is on his way. Just head back to where the rest of the company's camped. We should be back there by the time you arrive."

"Sure. Nate, like the lieutenant says, goin' home would be the best thing for you. Right now you're at loose ends. A lot of bad things have happened to you. You need to go home and be with your kinfolks. Trust me and Bob, it's for the best."

"I guess maybe you're right," Nate conceded.

"You'll see we are," Bob said. "Now, we've got to tend to the buryin', so we can get back on the trail."

***

Three graves had been dug by the Rangers the night before, under the same dying cottonwood where Nathaniel's wound had been treated. A fourth, shallow grave, unmarked and five hundred yards distant, already held the body of the dead outlaw. Nathaniel's mother, father, and brother lay alongside the open graves, their bodies wrapped in blankets.

The Rangers and Nathaniel gathered somberly around the open graves. Jim and Ed carefully lowered first Marcus, then Adele, and finally Jonathan into their final resting places. The Rangers removed their hats and stood while their Lieutenant gave a short prayer.

"Lord," he began, "Ain't none of us here really church-goin' men, but we all believe in You, and that someday we'll be with You in Heaven. We know not Your ways, but we are certain that Marcus, Adele, and Jonathan Stewart are with You right now, in the peace of Your love and mercy. Grant them eternal rest. We also pray that You keep their son and brother Nathaniel safe, and help guide him in this time of his trials. Amen."

"Amen," the Rangers and Nathaniel echoed.

"And Lord, if You could help us bring the outlaws who murdered these innocent people to justice, we'd sure appreciate that. Amen."

"Amen."

"Guess there's nothing else to say, Lord. Amen."

"Amen."

"Nate." Bob gave Nathaniel several clods of earth. Nathaniel tossed those on each of the bodies, then the Rangers filled in the graves. Crude wooden crosses with the names of the deceased were placed at the head of each. Once that was done, the Rangers, except for Jeb, saddled their horses, mounted up and rode off. Jeb placed an arm around Nathaniel's shoulders.

"C'mon, Nate. It's time to go."

He led Nathaniel to where his paint gelding waited, already saddled and bridled and tied to the sole corral post which had survived the fire.

"Nate, this here's Dudley," he said. "Named him after a

favorite uncle of mine." He patted the horse's shoulder. "Dudley, this here's Nate. He's gonna be ridin' with us for a spell. He's just lost his family, so you treat him gentle, hear?"

Dudley snorted and nuzzled Jeb's hand.

"He gonna be able to carry both of us?" Nathaniel asked.

"Dudley's a tough ol' bronc. He can carry double for quite a ways. He'll be just fine. C'mon, we might as well get a move on."

Jeb climbed into the saddle, then held out his left hand to Nathaniel.

"C'mon, Nate. Just swing your leg over Dudley's rump and settle down behind me. Wrap your arms around my waist to hang on."

"I dunno," Nate said.

"You sure don't want to walk all the way to San Saba, do you?"

"No, I guess I don't."

"Then get up here with me."

"All right." Nathaniel took Jeb's hand, and, with the Ranger's help, scrambled onto Dudley's back, just behind the saddle. As instructed, he wrapped his arms around Jeb's waist, holding on for dear life.

"Hey, take it easy there," Jeb pleaded. "I can't breathe, and you're squeezin' my belly so tight my guts are liable to pop out my backside. You don't have to hold on so tight, Nate. Just relax and feel the horse's motion. You'll be just fine."

"If you say so. I'll try." Nathaniel loosened his grip just a bit. Jeb took in a deep breath.

"There, that's better. I can get air in my lungs again. Dudley, let's go."

He heeled the paint into a walk and pointed his nose east, toward San Saba.

4

Two hours later, they rode into San Saba. On the way Nathaniel had resigned himself to being called Nate, the new, shortened version of his name the Rangers had given him. In fact, he kind of liked it.

"There's a doctor just a few blocks up the street, Nate," Jeb said. "He's treated some of us Rangers before. He's a good man, so we'll stop there first and have your head examined. Wait a minute, that don't sound quite right. Makes it seem as if you're loco. We'll have him look at the bullet gash on your scalp."

Despite himself, Nate gave a low chuckle. A few minutes later, Jeb reined up in front of a small whitewashed cottage. A sign out front read "Doctor Elijah Mannion".

"Just slide off Dudley's rump," Jeb told Nate. "Don't worry, he won't kick you."

Nate did as told, but grabbed Dudley's tail on the way down. The paint planted a hoof solidly in Nate's belly, knocking him halfway across the street. Nate lay there, curled up, hands clamped to his middle while he struggled for air. His eyes watered from the effort and pain. Jeb jumped off his horse and hurried up to him.

"Nate! You all right?"

"I thought... you said... your horse wouldn't... kick me," Nate gasped.

"Well, I never expected you to latch onto his tail," Jeb answered. "Any horse'll kick if you do that, no matter how mild-mannered he is. C'mon, let's get you to the doc. I'll help you up."

Jeb took Nate's hand and pulled him to his feet. With Nate walking hunched over, short of breath and hands still pressed to his belly, they headed inside.

"We're lucky. Nobody else here," Jeb said. The waiting room was empty.

"I'll be right with you," a voice called from the back room. A moment later, Dr. Elijah Mannion appeared. He was middle-aged, with a long salt-and-pepper beard. His eyes were deep blue and had a kindly appearance.

"Well, well, what have we here?" he asked.

"Mornin' doc," Jeb said. "You probably don't remember me, but I'm Ranger Jeb Rollins. You dug a bullet out of my back some months back. Got a boy with me who needs lookin' at. Name's Nate Stewart."

"I see. Ate too many green apples, did you son? And fell out of the tree getting them?"

Nate was still hunched over, holding his middle.

"No, doc. Dunno where you'd find an apple tree within two hundred miles of here anyway," Jeb answered. "He got kicked by a horse. That's not why we're here, though. He's got a bullet crease under those bandages. One of my pards patched him up, but it needs to be looked at."

"All right. Come with me and I'll have a look at him."

They followed Mannion into his examination room.

"Sit on that table, son," he ordered. Once Nate was settled, Mannion removed the bandages from his head.

"I'm going to clean this wound up just a bit. It may sting."

"It can't hurt any more than when it was stitched," Nate said.

"You're certainly right about that." Mannion took two bottles and some cloths from a shelf.

"How did you get this wound, Nate?" he asked as he worked on the boy.

Jeb answered instead. "Outlaws attacked his folks' ranch a few miles west of here. Killed his ma, pa, and older brother. Only reason Nate survived is they thought he was dead."

"That's a real shame. Outlaw bands will be the ruination of

Texas yet. I don't suppose you Rangers captured any of those men."

"The rest of my patrol is on their trail right now. Might even have caught up with 'em. I stayed behind to help Nate, here. He's got no kin left in Texas, so he's going back home to Delaware. He's got an aunt and uncle and a bunch of cousins there. That head wound ain't gonna keep him from travelin', is it?"

"Not at all," Mannion answered. "Your partner did as competent a job of treating this wound as most physicians, and better than many. Nate, I'm merely going to apply a fresh dressing and new bandages. Before I do that, however, I want to make certain your brain hasn't been concussed." He held up his hand.

"How many fingers do you see?"

"Two."

"That's right. Now, I'm going to look at your eyes."

Mannion examined both of Nate's eyes thoroughly, looking for signs of non-responsiveness or dilated or mismatched pupils.

"You appear not to have suffered any trauma to your brain. Have you experienced any dizziness? Have you kept falling asleep, even just dozing off?"

"No, sir."

"Good, good. How about nausea, the feeling that you need to throw up?"

"Not until Jeb's horse kicked me in the belly."

"Well, that's enough to make any man sick to his stomach. As long as you haven't vomited any blood, I don't believe any real harm was done. However, I do want to check your abdomen, so could you take off your shirt?"

"All right." Nate peeled off his borrowed shirt. Already a purple bruise was spreading across his belly where Jasper's hoof had struck. Mannion looked at that for just a moment.

"Lie back please, Nate," he requested.

"All right." Nate stretched out on the table. Mannion poked and prodded at his belly, pounding it lightly with the side of his fist at several points.

"Does that hurt here?"

"No, sir."

"How about here? And here? Any sharp pain?"

"No, sir."

"Good. I'd say you have nothing but a bad bruise, son. It should clear up in a few days. However, if you feel any sudden sharp, stabbing pains or begin vomiting blood come back here immediately. You can sit up and put your shirt back on now, then I'll finish up."

Mannion efficiently finished treating the wound to Nate's head.

"There, I'm all done. You'll need to have the stitches removed in a few days. Any doctor can do that for you. Just remember, if you feel any nausea or can't stay awake, you get right back here. Understood?"

"Yes, sir."

"Thanks, Doc," Jeb said. "How much do we owe you?"

"A dollar will cover it, Ranger."

"That's more than fair." Jeb dug in his pocket, pulled out a silver dollar, and gave it to Mannion.

"Nate, please accept my deepest sympathies on the loss of your family," Mannion said. "And I wish you Godspeed on your journey home. The Rangers are good men. I'm certain they'll bring the outlaws who murdered your family to justice."

"Thank you, sir."

"Nate, we've got a lot of things to do before the day's over," Jeb said. "Doc, *muchas gracias. Adios.*"

"Goodbye to you, Ranger. Nate, make sure to take care of yourself."

***

Jeb and Nate's next stop was the San Saba County Bank. A young teller there hesitated about granting Jeb's request to meet with the bank president, until Jeb pulled his silver star in silver circle badge from his pocket and pinned it to his vest. Five minutes later, they were seated in Homer Funston's office.

"Ranger Rollins, it's a pleasure to meet you," he said. "Would you care for a cigar?"

"No, thank you, Mr. Funston. Most of my pards smoke, but I never got into the habit."

"Fine, fine. You won't mind if I do." Funston chose a cigar from the jar on his desk, lit it, and drew a few puffs. He blew a ring of smoke toward the ceiling.

"Now, what can I do for the Texas Rangers?"

"This here's Nate Stewart. His family had a ranch a few miles west of here. Outlaws attacked the place, murdered everyone except Nate, and burned it to the ground. Nate's headed back home to Delaware. We're here to see what money his father might've had deposited in your bank. Since Nate's the sole survivor, it's his now."

"Of course, of course. Nate, please let me say how sorry I am for your loss. What was your father's first name?"

"It was Marcus. My mom's was Adele, and my brother's was Jonathan."

"Thank you. Miriam."

Funston called to the woman in the nearest teller's cage.

"Yes, Mr. Funston?"

"Could you bring me the records on the Marcus Stewart family accounts, please?"

"Right away, Mr. Funston."

"While we're waiting, Ranger Rollins, I can tell Nate that his father owned his ranch free and clear. He was one of the fortunate persons in that regard. I know it's a bit soon to ask, but since it will be your land, son, do you think you'd want to keep it or sell it? In either case, since you're a minor, you'll need a conservator to take care of the legal aspects. Do you understand what I'm saying?"

"Not really, sir."

"He's sayin' someone'll need to handle your money until you're of legal age, Nate," Jeb explained. "You'll need someone to make sure the taxes on your land are paid, things like that, until you decide what to do with it. And would I be correct in assuming you're offering to take on that job, Mr. Funston?"

"If Nate is agreeable, yes. Of course, if he has someone else in mind, or would prefer the court name someone…"

"What do you think, Nate?"

"I dunno, Jeb. I never had to think about… about…"

"Enough said for now. Mr. Funston, I reckon we'll wait on that decision for a spell."

"That's certainly understandable, Ranger. Ah, here's Miriam with the accounts now. Thank you, Miriam."

The secretary handed Funston the Stewart account records. He looked them over for a moment, then leaned back in his chair.

"Nate, as I seemed to recollect, your father had made several withdrawals from his account in the past few months. He needed to do that to keep the ranch going, until he was able to sell some of his cattle. Nonetheless, there is still several hundred dollars in the account. That will all be yours, of course, once everything works its way through the courts. I will need an address where to reach you."

"Mr. Funston, the renegades who murdered Nate's family left him with nothing but the clothes on his back," Jeb said. "In fact, they didn't even leave him all those. His shirt was gone when we found him. That's a borrowed one he's wearin'. Any chance you could bend the rules a bit, and let him have enough money from the account to buy some new duds? He's also gonna need money for stage and train tickets back home, and meal money besides."

"That could be a problem, but I can certainly try."

"How about if I agreed to make you my, what was it?" Nate asked.

"Your conservator? That might speed things up a bit. And if you are worried I may loot the account you need not fear about that. I'm a hard businessman, but a fair one. Your affairs will be safe in my hands. Ask anyone in town if you like."

"All right. You're in charge of my money, Mr. Funston."

"Excellent. You won't be sorry, Nate."

"But *you* will be if a nickel of the boy's money disappears, Funston," Jeb warned. "The Rangers will make sure of that. And it still doesn't solve our problem. Nate needs cash now, not later."

Funston pulled a gold pocket watch out of his vest and glanced at it.

"Judge Stanton should be at the courthouse right now. If we hurry over there, we should catch him before he heads out to dinner. We can have the necessary papers drawn up and signed. Then I can arrange a withdrawal for you, Nate. Will that do?"

"I guess so."

"Are you certain, Nate?"

"Yeah. Yeah, I am, Jeb."

"All right. Mr. Funston, let's go."

***

Realizing Nate was in a difficult situation, it didn't take long for Judge Stanton to prepare the necessary paperwork, have it signed, witnessed, and filed. Shortly after that was done, Nate left the bank with enough money to purchase a new outfit, as well as a stage ticket to Waco, from where he would make train connections home to Delaware. The stage would not be leaving for three days, so he and Jeb would be staying in San Saba until then.

"I have to stop by the marshal's office and let him know there's a Ranger in town. We generally let the local law know when we're around. After that I reckon our next stop should be the general store to get you some decent clothes, Nate," Jeb said. "It's just down the street. We'll stop there, then grab some chuck. After that we'll head for the barber shop for haircuts and baths for both of us, and a shave for me. Been a long time since I've had the chance to scrub the trail dust out of my hide. And we're both lookin' pretty shaggy. Once all that's done, we'll put up Dudley at the livery and figure out a place to stay." Like most cowboys, Jeb hated to walk, so would use his horse to complete

41

their errands, then stable him. "Does that sound all right to you?"

"I guess so," Nate answered.

"Nate, I know this is a lot for you right now, but you're handlin' everything pretty well. Just remember if you need to talk you go right ahead. I'll be listenin'."

"Thanks, Jeb. I'll be okay, I guess."

"You will be. You're a tougher kid than you realize, Nate. It'll take time, but you'll do all right. I'd bet my hat on it. Let's get to the store. I don't know about you, but I'm gettin' hungry."

"So am I."

"Good. We'll buy those clothes, then eat."

***

Jeb helped Nate pick out two pairs of denims, two shirts, a pair of sturdy boots, a red silk neckerchief, two sets of underwear, two pairs of socks, and a black Stetson. Once the purchases were completed, paid for, and wrapped, they headed for a nearby café for dinner of beefsteaks, boiled potatoes, and black eyed peas, with apple pie for dessert. After that, they crossed the street to the barber shop. A bell attached to the door jingled merrily when they opened it.

"C'mon in, gents," the barber greeted them. He glanced at the badge on Jeb's vest. "Ranger, huh? Reckon you're here for a shave and a haircut, from the looks of you."

"For me and the boy both. Baths also. I'm Jeb, and this here's Nate. I know it'll be tough workin' around the bandage on his head, so just trim him up as best you can."

"Sure, of course. I'm Bret Mason. What happened to you son? If you don't mind my askin'."

Nate swallowed hard before replying.

"Outlaws attacked our ranch. They killed my ma and pa and brother. I got shot and left for dead."

"Some of us Rangers have been trailin' that bunch for quite a while now. Came up on Nate's place a little too late to help his folks," Jeb added. "Rest of my patrol's still after 'em. With any luck they've caught 'em by now. I came with Nate to help him get his affairs in order. He's got no kin left in Texas, so he's goin' back home to Delaware to live with his aunt and uncle."

"I'm sure sorry to hear that, son," Mason said. "My prayers will be with you. Won't be much, but mebbe a trim and hot bath will make you feel a little better. Ranger, who's goin' first, you or the boy?"

"Take care of Nate first. It won't take as long to trim his hair as it will for my shearin' and shave."

"All right. I've already got some water heated. Let me get a couple more kettles started, then I'll start in on your hair, Nate."

Mason disappeared into the back room, then returned a few minutes later.

"Hop in the chair, Nate. By the time I'm done, your bath will be ready."

Mason worked carefully on the boy so as not to cause him any further pain from the bullet wound. He looked at Nate critically once he was done.

"Not too bad, considerin'," he said. He held up a mirror for Nate to look in. "What do you think, Nate?"

"No, it's not. In fact, it's just fine."

"Good. Now follow me and I'll finish gettin' your bath ready."

Mason removed the cloth protecting Nate's clothes and brushed off his neck and shoulders. He led Nate into the back room, where he poured more hot water into a large zinc tub.

"Soap, washcloth, and towels are on the chair next to the tub," he said. "More towels on the shelf if you need 'em. Just be careful you don't get those bandages wet. You don't want water soakin' through to the stitches. You can hang your clothes on those pegs. Those new duds in that package?"

"Yeah. I needed to replace the ones I lost when our ranch was burned."

"Just leave those on the shelf until you're ready to get dressed. Take as long as you like."

"All right. And thanks, Mr. Mason."

"No need to thank me, son. It's the least I can do."

Once the barber left, Nate stripped out of his dirty clothes and stepped into the tub. He settled as deeply as possible into the steaming hot water, letting it soak aches from his body and grime from his skin. As he lay there, a feeling of deep sadness came over him. After a while, he realized it was more than just the loss of his parents and brother. He now understood what was troubling him. Despite his previous dislike for Texas, he now knew it was home. He had no desire to return to Delaware. And he wanted to be there when the men who had killed his parents and brother were brought to justice. With a sigh, he settled even more deeply into the tub. As Lieutenant Berkeley and Jeb had said, there was no future for him in the Lone Star State. Like it or not, he would need to go back to Wilmington.

***

"Boy howdy, you look good in those new clothes, Nate," Jeb said as they headed for the livery stable after their baths and haircuts. "That hat'll fit you better once those bandages come off. Just too bad we couldn't find any Eastern-type clothes for you. You're lookin' like a real cowpuncher."

"That's all right, Jeb. My friends back in Delaware all thought I was gonna be a cowboy. This way when I get home, I'll at least look like one."

"That's the spirit. Nate, Ranger pay ain't all that much, so we can't often afford a hotel room. I can usually talk the hostler at the stable to let me sleep in the loft for a couple extra bits a night. Besides, I like to stay close to my horse. You mind doin' that? If not, you could use some of your money to get yourself a room for the next couple of nights."

"No, sleepin' in the loft will be okay," Nate said. "It'll probably be a lot more comfortable than crowdin' into a bed with two of three of my cousins once I get back home."

"Then that's what we'll do. After Dudley's in a stall and fed, it'll be time to think about our supper. You about ready to chow down again?"

"Now that you mention it, yeah. But I'm also real tired."

"You've been through a lot. We'll get supper, then turn in early."

***

With nothing to do until the stage arrived in two days, Nate and Jeb had little to do the next day. Most of the time they spent sitting on barrels in front of the stable, watching people as they walked by. Nate grew more quiet as the day went on.

"Nate, you feelin' all right?" Jeb asked. "Your head ain't botherin' you, is it?"

"No, not at all," Nate said.

"How about your belly? You seem to be eatin' all right, but is that kick from Dudley gettin' worse?"

"No, it's fine, except for the funny purple color it turned where Dudley got me."

"I'm sure sorry about that, but I'll bet you'll never grab a horse's tail again."

"You can be certain I won't. Dudley taught me a good lesson. No, I'm okay. Just feelin' kind of down."

"Well, that's understandable, with all you've been through. Losin' a family like you did would throw a man twice your age. You'll start to feel better once you're with kinfolks. Things'll never be the same, but the hurt will lessen with time. Meantime, you ready for supper?"

"I guess so."

***

Nate merely picked at his meal that night. When he and Jeb bedded down in the stable's hay loft, he lay staring at the roof for quite some time.

"Jeb, you awake?" he finally whispered.

"Yeah. I'm still awake," Jeb answered. "Why?"

"I've gotta tell you something. I don't want to go back to Delaware. I want to stay here, in Texas."

***

45

Jeb and Nate spent the entire next day trying to figure out how the boy could remain in Texas. By the end of the day, they still came up empty. A feeling of hopelessness settled over Nate. It looked like he would be getting on the stage the next afternoon.

"Tell you what, Nate," Jeb said, about eight that night. "Sometimes I can think better over a beer or two. Let's go to the Dusty Trail Saloon. I'll buy you a couple of sarsaparillas, we can get some ham and eggs, and mebbe we'll come up with somethin'."

"All right. Maybe you can buy me a beer, too."

"Mebbe I *can't*," Jeb retorted. "You're way too young for red-eye. Don't get any ideas from the ladies in there, either. There'll be time enough for those in a couple of years."

"It was worth a try," Nate said, with a grin.

"There. That's better. You're smilin'," Jeb said. "Let's go."

It was only two blocks to the Dusty Trail, so rather than saddle Dudley, Jeb decided to walk. When they entered the saloon, it was mostly empty. A few men stood at the bar, several were playing games of chance, and one or two were talking with the percentage girls. A short, stocky, lantern-jawed cowboy, with brown hair tending to gray under his hat, was sitting at one of the tables, working on a bottle of whiskey. He nodded at the Ranger as Jeb walked by. Jeb nodded in return, then he and Nate bellied up to the bar.

"Evenin', Ranger," the bartender said. "I'm Joe Hardy, the owner of this fine establishment. What's your pleasure?"

"Beer for me, sarsaparilla for the boy," Jeb ordered.

"Comin' right up." A moment later, a mug of beer and bottle of pop were placed on the bar in front of them.

"Just call when you're ready for another," Hardy said.

"Will do," Jeb answered.

Jeb only gave the saloon a quick glance. He'd been in dozens of others just like this one, all over Texas. There was the mirror-backed bar, the paintings of cattle drives and scantily clad women on the walls, the games of chance; poker, faro, chuck-a-luck and roulette, and the out of tune piano. Tobacco smoke swirled around the coal-oil chandeliers. The entire place smelled of tobacco smoke, spilled whiskey, and sweat.

However, Nate had never even peeked into a saloon, let alone been inside one. He kept glancing around, looking from one end to the other, taking in the entire room. Try as he might, he could not avert his gaze from the percentage girls in their low-cut dresses.

"Try to keep your eyes in your head, boy," Jeb ordered, with a laugh. Nate blushed bright red.

Jeb was working on his second beer and Nate on his third sarsaparilla when five men entered the saloon. Jeb glanced at their image in the back-bar mirror and stiffened. He turned to face the newcomers.

"Nate, get over in the corner," he ordered.

"Why? What's wrong, Jeb?"

"Just listen to me. Get over in the corner, now!"

Nate edged away from the bar.

"Trouble, Ranger?" the stocky cowboy asked.

"Nothin' I can't handle," Jeb answered.

"I'm not so sure about that. I think I might have to take a hand in this game," the cowboy replied.

"Appreciate the offer, but this is Ranger business. And five to one odds are just about right."

The newcomers were now halfway across the room.

"Hold it right there, Stevenson," Jeb ordered. "Rest of your boys, too. Keep your hands away from your guns, less'n you want to eat some lead."

The leader of the group stopped short.

"Well, well, if it ain't Ranger Jeb Rollins," he said, with a sneer. "Of all the rotten luck."

"I'd call it *good* luck, Stevenson," Jeb said. "The Rangers have been lookin' for you and your bunch for quite a spell. Your cattle rustlin' and horse-thievin' days are over. You're under arrest, all of you. Just shuck those gunbelts and raise your hands, nice and easy-like."

"You really are a barrel of laughs, you know that, Ranger? Here we are, five of us and one of you, and you really believe you're gonna take us all in. I don't think so. We'll be keepin' our guns."

"Make that *two* of us, mister," the stocky cowboy said. He came to his feet, his hand hovering over the butt of the six-gun on his right hip. His face was set in hard lines, his dark eyes grim and determined.

Sensing trouble about to start, most of the patrons and employees of the saloon scrambled to get out of the line of fire, seeking cover behind posts or under tables. Several fled out the front door.

"I told you to stay out of this, cowboy," Jeb said.

"Thought I'd even up the odds a little."

"Still got you both outnumbered," Stevenson snapped. With that, he went for his gun.

Jeb already had his gun out and leveled by the time Stevenson cleared leather. He put a bullet into Stevenson's chest, slamming him back.

Powdersmoke filled the Dusty Trail as Stevenson's partners, along with the cowboy, pulled their guns and blazed away at each other. A bullet burned along Jeb's ribs, then he shot one of Stevenson's men in the right breast, spinning him to the floor.

Another of Stevenson's men went down when the cowboy shot him just above his belt buckle. The man dropped his gun, clawed at his bullet-torn gut, jackknifed, and fell to the sawdust covered floor, howling in pain. Then a bullet caught the cowboy in his left thigh, dropping him to one knee. The man who shot him then turned his gun on Jeb. Concentrating on the other man still standing, Jeb didn't see the outlaw thumb back the hammer of his pistol, ready to put a bullet into the Ranger's side.

Nate jumped from the corner where he had taken shelter and hit the outlaw in a long, diving tackle, driving his head into the man's ribs and knocking him off his feet. The outlaw's gun spilled from his hand, firing when it hit the floor, the bullet harmlessly ripping a long splinter out of the front of the bar. Both Nate and the outlaw scrambled after the gun. Nate managed to reach it first, grabbed it, and clubbed the barrel on the base of the outlaw's neck. The man stiffened, groaned, and slumped to the floor, out cold.

Two last shots were fired, and the final member of the gang toppled to the sawdust with two bullets in his chest, one from Jeb's Peacemaker, the other from the cowboy's .44 Remington.

Silence descended on the saloon, broken only by the moaning of the wounded outlaw and the curses of the cowboy as he struggled to his feet. Gun still at the ready, Jeb quickly checked the outlaws. Three were dead, the wounded man had passed out, and the one Nate had clubbed lay still as death, his breathing ragged. Nate was kneeling alongside him, still holding the outlaw's gun. His gaze was fixed on the pistol.

"Nate. You all right?" Jeb asked. There was no response. "Nate!"

Nate didn't answer. He kept staring at the gun.

"Nate!" Jeb shook the boy's shoulder. "You all right, son? Good work handlin' this hombre. I reckon you just saved my life. I'm obliged to you."

"Huh? Oh. Yeah, I think I'm okay. Jeb, this is my brother's gun."

"What?"

"This is Jonathan's gun."

"Are you certain?"

"Yes. I'm positive. Look at the handle. See, right there. Jonathan burned his initials into it."

"Let me see that." Jeb took the gun from Nate. As he had said, the initials "JAS" were burned into both of the Smith and Wesson's walnut grips.

The cowboy came limping over to Jeb and Nate. His right pants leg was dark with blood.

"The boy all right, Ranger?" he asked.

"Yeah, he's fine. How about yourself?" Jeb answered.

"I'll be okay. Slug just took a chunk of flesh outta my leg. I'll patch myself up. My name's Carl, by the way. Carl Swan. And what about you? Looks like you caught a slug yourself."

The left side of Jeb's shirt was also wet with fresh blood.

"Jeb Rollins. Bullet just pinked my ribs. Appreciate your help. The boy here's Nate Stewart. His family was all killed a few days back by a bunch we Rangers have been chasin'. Looks like this hombre might've been one of 'em. This here gun belonged to Nate's brother, Jonathan."

"That's my brother's gunbelt he's wearin' too," Nate said.

"Oh, it is, is it? Let's just find out where he got it," Jeb answered. He rolled the unconscious outlaw onto his back, unbuckled the gunbelt from around his waist and slid it off him. He handed it to Nate.

"Time this got back to its rightful owner. It's yours now. Hardy!"

"Yeah, Ranger?" the bartender answered.

"Bring me some water. Time to rouse this coyote."

"Sure, Ranger. Comin' right up."

Before Hardy could bring the water, the batwings swung open and the San Saba marshal, Jock Holmes, walked in. He held a double-barreled sawn off shotgun at the ready. He quickly took in the scene, the five men lying on the floor, four of them dead or dying, the patrons standing around, not daring to move, and the two men and a boy alongside one of the downed men.

"Don't anyone move," he ordered. "Just what in the Sam Hill's goin' on in here?"

"Everything's under control, Marshal," Jeb said. "Just had a bit of a ruckus is all."

"Oh, it's you, Ranger," Holmes said. "I might've known. What exactly happened?"

"Man lyin' over there is Mort Stevenson. He's wanted for cattle rustlin' and horse thievin'... or I reckon I should say he *was* wanted, bein' as he's in no shape to ever steal another horse or cow. Rest of these men are his pardners. When I tried to arrest 'em, they objected."

"I see. Mistake on their part."

Holmes glanced at the wounded Swan.

"Carl, how'd you get yourself plugged? Mixin' in where you don't belong again? Someday your nosiness is gonna get you killed."

"Hey, the Ranger was outnumbered five to one. I evened up the odds a little, that's all. Got me one of them renegades, too. Plugged him dead center, right in the belly. And shot another one, along with the Ranger."

"It'd probably be me lyin' there in the sawdust rather than these outlaws if Carl hadn't taken a hand," Jeb answered. "So, you've got no call to hassle him, Marshal. Now, as far as mistakes, this hombre here was carryin' Nate's brother's gun. That's a mistake which could get him hung. I was about to wake him up and ask where he got that six-gun when you walked in."

"Don't let me stop you. I'm a mite curious about that myself."

"All right. Hardy, where's that water?"

"Right here, Ranger." He handed a mug to Jeb. "Only it's not water, it's beer. That was a bit handier."

"Seems a shame to waste perfectly good beer," Jeb said, with a shrug, "but here goes."

He poured the beer over the outlaw's face. The man came to, spluttering.

"What the...?"

His curse was cut short when he realized he was staring into the barrel of Jeb's Peacemaker, which the Ranger held three feet from his nose, aimed right between his eyes.

"Just hold it right there, Mister, or I'll finish what Nate started. You've got some questions to answer, and you'd better come up with the right ones, real quick."

"Mort?"

"He's dead. So's the rest of your pards, except one, and he don't have long. And you're lookin' at a noose, so they might be better off than you are."

"What're you talkin' about, Ranger?" Despite the gun pointed at him, the outlaw tried to sit up, but fell back with a groan.

51

"Ow! My head. What'd that kid hit me with?"

"His brother's gun. The gun you were carryin'. The gun that's gonna put the rope around your neck and pull it tight."

"You're loco, Ranger. You tryin' to say I killed that kid's brother?"

"That's exactly what I'm sayin'. His folks' ranch was attacked a few days back. His ma, pa, and brother were killed. Place was stripped clean of cattle and anything valuable then burned to the ground. The gun you were carryin' was taken off his dead brother."

"You can't prove that."

"Oh, yes I can. First of all, it's a Smith and Wesson American cartridge revolver. There's not many of those in these parts."

"That doesn't mean anythin'. There's still more than one of those in Texas."

"Mebbe that's true. But the man you killed was named Jonathan Stewart. He burned his initials into the grips of that gun. That's all the proof I need to tie you to his murder. Or mebbe I'll just let the kid take care of you. You'd like another crack at him, wouldn't you, Nate?"

"I reckon I would, at that."

"I wouldn't mind takin' him out behind this saloon, either," Carl added.

Sweat broke out on the man's brow.

"Now, hold on just a minute. I didn't kill anybody, and I sure didn't attack this kid's ranch. Sure, I'll admit to rustlin', but I never took to killin'. I *bought* that gun."

"You got any way of provin' that? And just what is your name, anyway?"

"It's Hawkins. Bob Hawkins. I bought the gun from an hombre who was with an outfit trailin' a small herd of longhorns southeast three-four days ago."

"My dad's cattle," Nate exclaimed. "Guess that means the Rangers didn't find 'em yet."

"Mebbe, mebbe not," Jeb answered. "Men like the ones who attacked your place hit fast, get rid of the stolen beeves or horses quick as they can, then move on."

"But if one of 'em had Jonathan's gun..."

"I'll admit it doesn't look good," Jeb conceded. "Most likely they got away from the boys somehow. We'll find 'em, though. I promise you that. Hawkins," he continued, "You got a name for this hombre you supposedly bought the gun from? And a description?"

"I never met him before. Only have a first name, Manny. Looks to be half-white, half-Mexican. Ridin' with eight other men. The one who appeared to be leadin' the outfit was a scary-lookin' dude. Real skinny and pale complexioned, hair so blonde it was almost white. Fancy dresser, too. Wore two matched pearl-handled .45 Colt Armies. His eyes were a real pale blue, and when he looked at you they'd freeze the blood right in your veins. If'n I didn't know better I'd swear he's a ghost, or someone back from the grave."

"And they let your bunch just ride straight up to 'em? I'm findin' that hard to swallow, Hawkins."

"They didn't do that, no sir. We just stumbled onto 'em, that's all. They were headin' south and we were headin' north. Came upon 'em in an *arroyo* the trail runs through about forty miles southwest of here. Mort seemed to know the leader, but he didn't make any introductions. You know how it is, Ranger. You don't ask questions."

"All right, Hawkins. You can get up. Slow and easy."

"You believe me, Ranger?"

"I reckon. But you're still facin' a long stretch behind bars for rustlin'. However, it looks like you won't hang, so as they say, no noose is good noose."

Carl and Marshal Holmes winced.

"Ranger, you oughtta be gut-shot for that joke," Carl said.

Dr. Mannion had arrived and examined the shot men while Hawkins was being questioned.

"What's the verdict, doc?" Holmes asked.

"Three of 'em are dead. One's belly shot. I can try to save him, but it's not likely." Mannion looked at Jeb and Carl. "Looks like you two need treating also."

"They're just scratches," Jeb said.

"Scratches which could become gangrenous and lead to blood poisoning," Mannion answered. "Come by my office just so I can check you both out."

"All right," Jeb said. "Soon as we get this hombre behind bars where he belongs. Hawkins, let's go."

Stevenson and his men had tied their horses in front of the Dusty Trail. When Nate, following Jeb and his prisoner, stepped outside one of the mounts lifted its head and whickered. Nate stopped short.

"Red?"

The horse whickered again, more loudly.

"Big Red! It is you." Nate walked up to the horse, who nuzzled his cheek.

"That sorrel your brother's horse, Nate?" Jeb asked.

"He sure is," Nate answered. "That's his saddle, too. Just like his gun, Jonathan burned his initials into the saddle."

"Looks like you weren't tellin' me the entire truth, Hawkins," Jeb said. "Were you ridin' that sorrel?"

"Yeah. Yeah, I was. But I got him from the same fella who sold me the gun. Traded my bay for him. Thought I got the better part of the deal, since my horse was plumb wore out. Guess I was wrong."

"I'd say so," Jeb answered. "Unless you can prove you didn't know that horse was stolen, you might still be facin' the noose.

***

Once Hawkins was safely behind bars, Jeb, Nate, and Carl went to Dr. Mannion's office. Mannion was still working on the outlaw Carl had shot, so they had to wait to have their own wounds treated.

"I have to say I'm much obliged to the both of you," Jeb said. "If you hadn't stepped in, I'd be headed for Boot Hill right about now."

"Don't even mention it, Ranger," Carl said. "I'm more than

happy to see thievin' skunks like that get what's comin' to 'em."

"Nevertheless, I'm grateful. And Nate, you showed a lot of grit back in that saloon. I think you just got yourself a new job."

"What do you mean, Jeb? I thought you couldn't come up with any."

"I couldn't, but *you* did. How'd you like to join the Texas Rangers?"

"What?"

"Well, not officially, of course. You're a mite too young. But I figure I can talk Cap'n Quincy into takin' you on as a camp helper. You see, me and the rest of the Rangers you met are part of an entire company of men. We're camped on the San Saba, two days ride southwest of here. We've got an old Ranger who's our camp cook. You'd be his helper, rustlin' up firewood, helpin' him cook and clean up, give him a hand with some of the chores. What do you think?"

"You really mean that?"

"I'd also add you could learn a lot about Rangerin' while you're with us. No guarantees that Cap'n Quincy will take you on, or how long the job will last, but if you'd like to take your chances rather'n headin' back to Delaware..."

"I'd take the job if I were you, Nate," Carl said.

"You took the words right out of my mouth. Carl. But Jeb, are you sure? I don't even know how to ride that good. Jonathan was the cowboy, not me."

"The only way to learn is by doin'," Jeb answered. "Which means the best way to learn how to handle a horse is by ridin' him. And we'll sure be doin' a lot of hard ridin' the next two days. You'll be sore, but I'd bet my hat you'll learn fast. You proved yourself today when you took on Hawkins. You're a man to ride the river with, Nate."

"Jim said the same thing too, about me and my brother. What's that mean, Jeb?"

"Ride the river with? That means you're a man who can be absolutely trusted, no matter how tough the goin' is or how dangerous a situation becomes. It comes from the cattle drives, where fordin' a herd of cows across a flooded river is about the most dangerous thing a man can face. If you can count on your pard, no matter what, he is a man to ride the river with."

"It's the highest praise you can get in Texas, son," Carl added. "And I wouldn't worry. You'll do just fine."

"So would you, Carl. You ever think about joinin' up with the Rangers?"

"Me? Heck no. I'm too hair-triggered. Also don't like bein' tied down to one outfit. But I appreciate the offer."

"Well, if you ever change your mind, just find the nearest Ranger company and sign on. Give 'em my name."

"I'll do that."

Doctor Mannion emerged from the back room.

"I've done all I can for that man," he said. "It's just a matter of time until he's gone. Carl, I'll take you next."

"All right."

Once Carl went in, Jeb turned to Nate.

"Since you're not goin' home after all, you need to write a letter to your aunt and uncle. They need to know what's happened. We'll mail it before we leave in the morning."

***

It was well after midnight before Jeb and Nate returned to the livery and settled down in the loft. Jeb quickly fell asleep, but Nate lay on his back, his mind racing. His emotions churned, from sadness at the loss of his family, to excitement at the thought of riding with the Texas Rangers, to fear deep in his gut. What if Captain Quincy wouldn't let him work as a helper? Or worse, what if he couldn't handle the job? Maybe he *should* just go back to Delaware. That would be the safe, sensible thing to do. No. He could never go back. Either he'd make good in Texas, or he'd die trying.

5

"What do you mean, you don't know how to saddle and bridle a horse?" Jeb asked Nate as they readied to leave San Saba just after nine the next morning. They had waited for the Post Office to open so Nate could mail the letter to his Aunt Ida and Uncle Henry, then stop at the general store for supplies. Now, they were at the livery stable. Nate had the blanket and saddle on Big Red's back, but was standing with the cinch in his hand, unsure how to fasten it.

"We never owned a horse back in Delaware. After Jonathan got Big Red he wanted to teach me how, but I never cared to learn," Nate explained. "Now I regret bein' so stubborn."

"Well, you're gonna have to learn, and right quick. Let me finish saddlin' up and I'll help you."

Jeb finished tightening the saddle on Dudley's back and came over to Nate.

"I know I checked Red's feet for you, so we won't worry about those," he said. "But tonight you're gonna get a lesson on how to care for your horse, Nate. Out here a man has to depend on his horse for his very life. That's why horse stealin' is a hangin' offense. If you steal a man's horse and leave him afoot, you might as well have signed his death warrant. Now here, let me show you. At least you've got the saddle on Red's back, rather'n under his belly." Jeb stopped and chuckled. "And you've got the saddle just about where it belongs. You should move it up a bit more over your horse's withers, though. That's this here high point above his shoulders." Jeb moved the saddle forward a couple of inches. "There, that's better. See how the saddle fits right over his withers? That helps keep it in place. You've got the cinch strap in your hand, looped through the cinch's buckle, and the cinch is under Red in just about the right spot. You pull up the strap into the buckle on the saddle, under the buckle then over it, then slide it to the left. So far so good, right?"

"Right, Jeb."

"Good. Now you bring the strap back around and over the front of the buckle, to the right. Bring it back under the buckle, keep it behind the loop you just made, then pull it down. That'll tighten it up. If there's too much strap left, you can either run it through the buckles on each end twice before makin' the knot, or just make a loop of the extra and tuck it in. Easy enough, right?"

"Seems to be."

"And it is, except for one thing you've always gotta watch out for. A lotta horses'll suck in air to blow up their belly when you're tightenin' the cinch. Then, when they let it out, the cinch ain't so tight around their belly. More comfortable for them. Problem with that is, with a loose cinch, the saddle'll slip sideways as soon as you step in the stirrup; or worse, it'll slip a bit later, while you're lopin' along. Next thing you know, you're on the ground, seein' stars, while your horse is runnin' off, kickin' at the saddle—which is now underneath him. He'll probably wreck the saddle, and you'll be facin' a long walk, if you didn't break your neck. You want your cinch to be tight, with just enough room so your horse can breathe easy."

"So, how do I stop him from blowin' up his belly?"

"There's a couple of ways. Lotta men'll either give their horse a kick or knee in the belly. That'll knock the air outta him, but I feel it's kinda cruel. When you spend as much time with your horse as us Rangers do, you want to be friends with him, not have him scared of you—or worse, fightin' you all the time. So what I do is, either circle him around a few times, or walk him a few steps. He'll naturally let the air out, then you can tighten the cinch. Watch."

58

Jeb led Red around him in a tight circle.

"See, now you can tighten the cinch just fine." He pulled on the cinch strap to take up the slack.

"Wow. That was really loose," Nate said.

"Which is why you always check your cinch twice before mountin' up. Now, you buckle the breast strap in place. That keeps the saddle from slidin' back. Then we have the back cinch. Some men only use one, but I see your brother used a double cinch. I prefer that too. Second cinch just keeps the saddle a little more stable if your horse bucks or you're ridin' over rough terrain. But you don't want to tighten that one as tight. It's not the main cinch keepin' the saddle in place. Since it's right by your horse's flanks, which are real sensitive, he won't tolerate it bein' too tight. Or if it's back too far, you pull it up and it hits his— um—privates, he's sure gonna take a buckin' fit. Now, Red's a gelding, so that's not quite the problem it would be if he were still a stud, but that back cinch in the wrong place could really be painful, as you can imagine."

Nate winced.

"There, the cinches are all set," Jeb continued. "Now, the bridle. That's real easy. You hold it up so the headstall is just in front of Red's ears. That's a good boy, Red. Then you slip the bit in his mouth."

"Won't he bite me?"

"Not if you do it right. Here, see this gap between his teeth?"

"Yeah."

"If he doesn't open his mouth, you slide your fingers in there, both sides. He'll open wide, and you slip the bit right in. It sits in that gap. Then you slide the headstall over his ears, buckle the throatlatch in place, and you're all set. Think you can do that next time?"

"I'm sure I can."

"Good. Now get up on Red, and I'll check the length of your stirrups."

Nate put his foot in the stirrup and swung up on Red's back. Once he settled in the saddle, his feet barely reached the top of the stirrups.

"Like I thought, they're too long for you. Your brother was taller, right?"

"Yeah, he was," Nate confirmed.

"You want your stirrups set so your knees are just slightly bent. Here, I'll adjust them for you."

Jeb shortened the left stirrup.

"There. How's that?"

"That feels fine."

"Good. I'll fix the other one, then we'll head on out."

Once Nate's stirrups were set, Jeb mounted his own horse. He urged Dudley into a walk.

"You want to keep your horse to a walk for a half-mile or so until he warms up, Nate," he explained. "Only time you make an exception to that is if you're in a real hurry, like if you're after a band of outlaws who've just robbed a bank, or say Comanches have discovered your camp and you need to outrun 'em. In that case, you get your horse movin' as fast as you can, right off."

Jeb glanced at Nate and pulled his paint to a stop.

"Hold on a minute."

"Why? What's wrong, Jeb?"

"Why're you holdin' your reins like that?"

Nate had a rein in each hand and his elbows sticking out.

"Isn't that how?"

"No, it's not. You take both reins in the left hand, or right if you happen to be left-handed, which you ain't. You can't fire a gun or toss a rope if both your hands are busy holdin' the reins. Make your hand into a fist. Let the reins lie in your palm. And don't have your elbows flappin' all over the place like a scarecrow."

Nate took the reins in his left hand, holding it just over the saddlehorn.

"How's this?"

"Much better. You might want to loosen up on the reins just a bit. A loose rein is generally easier on both you and your horse, unless he's actin' up. Now, you take the left rein and lay

60

it against the left side of his neck if you want him to turn right, or the right rein against the right if you want him to turn left. At the same time, press your knee against his side in the direction you want him to turn... left knee for a left turn, right for a right. You got that?"

"Yeah, I'm pretty sure I do."

"You'll get the hang of it. Easier to keep your balance if you look toward the horizon. And don't be admirin' your shadow while you ride. Shadow-riders only make a fool of themselves, sooner or later. By the time we reach camp, you'll either be a rider or you won't. Let's keep movin'."

Jeb out his paint into a walk once again. They had only gone a short distance when Nate's horse stopped. His tail lifted. Jeb rode on a few yards before he realized Nate was not keeping up. He turned and called to him.

"What're you stoppin' for now, Nate?"

"I didn't. Red did. He stopped to poop."

Sure enough, Big Red had just deposited a large, odiferous mound of manure in the middle of the trail.

"He doesn't need to stop to poop. Keep him movin' when he needs to go. Last thing you need is a horse that stops to poop when you're in the middle of a running gun battle. Only time you let your horse stop is when he needs to pee. In that case, stand up in your stirrups and lean forward. That takes pressure off his kidneys and makes it easier for him to go."

"What if we're in the middle of a runnin' gunfight or bein' chased by Indians when he needs to pee?"

"He's probably not gonna pee while he's runnin'," Jeb answered, with a chuckle, "But if he does, your legs are gonna get splashed. Now get him movin'. We've got a lot of ground to cover before nightfall."

Half a mile later, Jeb put Dudley into a jogtrot. Nate's horse matched the pace, then began to buck.

"Jeb!" Nate yelled.

"Stick with him, Nate. He's just feelin' good and workin' the kinks outta his back. Most horses do when they're startin' out and feelin' good. He'll stop in a minute." Underneath him, Dudley also let out a few well-timed bucks, then settled into a steady stride.

"See what I mean? You rode him just fine, pardner."

"Yeah. I did, didn't I?" Nate grinned from ear to ear.

A few minutes later, Jeb increased their pace to a lope, a gait which would cover a lot of ground quickly, yet still conserve the horses as much as possible. While they rode along, Nate's appreciation for the rugged beauty of Texas, which had escaped his notice until now, grew. The sky was a deep clear blue, not fouled by the smoke from the factories and DuPont's gunpowder plants like back in Wilmington. The land was level to gently rolling, sometimes cut by a dry wash or shallow ravine, and interspersed with an occasional low hill. The vegetation was mostly scrub brush and cactus, with mesquite that grew in many cases as large as small trees. Where they rode closer to the San Saba, there were cottonwoods, pin oaks, and junipers, even an infrequent cypress.

The further they rode, the more Nate felt as one with his horse. He had Jonathan's gunbelt buckled around his waist. The weight of the heavy Smith and Wesson on his right hip and the Bowie knife in the sheath on his left felt natural, as if they'd always belonged there. Jonathan's Winchester was also in the saddle boot.

If I ever want to be a Ranger, I'm gonna have to learn how to shoot that rifle, Nate thought. His reverie was interrupted by Jeb's voice.

"Nate, a man's gotta be aware of his surroundings at all times out here," Jeb said. "That goes double for a lawman, especially a Ranger, so I'm gonna teach you to read sign as much as I can while we're ridin'. See that fella up there?"

Jeb pointed to a large bird wheeling in the sky.

"He's a red-tailed hawk. And see those over there?"

He indicated several black birds circling and descending in the distance, off to the right.

"Yep, I see 'em."

"Those are buzzards. Somethin's dead in the brush out there. We'll ride over and take a looksee, just in case it's a human. Just keep in mind, birds can tell you a lot. A jay screamin' or flock of crows burstin' out of the trees means somethin's stirred 'em up, and that somethin' could well be a drygulcher waitin' to put a bullet in your back."

"All right. I'll remember that, Jeb."

They turned off the trail. When they reached the spot where the buzzards had landed the ugly black birds scattered, squawking in protest as they rose into the sky, their wings flapping.

"Well, that's not a man anyway, Nate," Jeb said. "It's a wild boar. You don't want to tangle with one of those. They've got bad eyesight, a nasty temper, and those tusks are razor sharp. They'll tear you to shreds. A wild boar ain't afraid of anythin', either. They'll charge a horse as quick as they'll charge a man. Sometimes you can empty your gun into one and it'll still keep a-comin'. Looks like this one ain't been dead all that long, so the meat ain't spoiled. I reckon it's time for dinner. You hungry?"

"My belly's been rumblin' for the past hour. But are you certain that pig's safe to eat?"

"Nate, think of that hog as manna from Heaven," Jeb answered. "Out here we've gotta rely on game for most of our meat, except for the bacon we carry. Least we didn't have to hunt for this meal. Tell you what. There's a small spring just over there. Why don't you take care of the horses while I cut some pork chops from that boar? Loosen their cinches so they're more comfortable, let 'em drink, then tie 'em to that mesquite. Leave 'em enough rope so they can reach the grass. Fill our canteens while you're there. I'll show you how to tie a horse so he can't break loose, but you can get him untied right quick."

"All right."

They dismounted. Jed unwrapped the end of Dudley's lead rope from his saddlehorn. Like most cowboys, he rode with a halter always on his horse's head, rope attached, in addition to the bridle. That made securing a horse much faster and easier, and the bridle could easily be slipped off for the horse's comfort.

"You take your rope like this," he said. "Loop it around the hitch rail, tree, fence, whatever you're tyin' your horse to. Then, you make a knot, like so." Jeb looped the rope around again. "It's almost like tyin' your cinch, only you bring the rope up and through, leavin' a loop in it. Now, if your horse decides to try'n break free, he can't. Pullin' back won't get him anywhere. But if you need to untie him in a hurry, you just tug on the end of the rope and it's untied. See?"

Jeb jerked the free end of the rope and the knot fell open.

"Sure. But what if your horse figures out by pullin' on the rope he can get loose?" Nate asked.

"Then you've got a mighty smart cayuse," Jeb answered, with a laugh. "And I've seen more'n one who's figured that out. In fact, my Dudley's one of 'em. In that case you can't use the slip knot. You just have to tie a good tight knot, or wrap the reins around whatever you're tyin' him to a couple of times. Think you've got the idea?"

"Yeah, it's pretty easy."

"Good. Take 'em for a drink."

Nate led the horses to the waterhole. By the time he finished letting them drink and tying them, Jeb had cut several chops from the boar, as well as a half dozen long strips from its belly.

"This here belly meat's where bacon comes from," he explained. "Now, this ain't been cured, so it's not exactly bacon, but it'll still be mighty tasty. Help me gather some wood and we'll start a fire."

There were plenty of dead mesquite twigs and branches lying around, so it didn't take long to gather enough for a fire. Once the wood was stacked, Jeb took a bundle of lucifers from his vest pocket, broke one off, and scratched it to life on his belt. He touched the match to some shavings, which quickly caught.

"I'm gonna show you how to start a fire with just a flint, Nate, but not today," he said. Soon the meat was sizzling in the pan, with coffee boiling in the pot alongside.

"Smells good, don't it, Nate?"

"My mouth's waterin' already. Sure hope it tastes as good as it smells."

"It will."

Once the meat was done, Jeb piled it high on the tin plates, and filled the tin mugs with thick, black coffee. He passed a plate and mug to Nate.

"Eat up, kid."

"Thanks, Jeb."

Nate dug into his food with relish. He downed two pork chops and tossed away the bones before he stopped. He started laughing.

"What's so funny, Nate?" Jeb asked. "Sure hope it ain't my cookin'."

"No, it's not that at all. I was just thinkin' what my ma would say if she saw me sittin' here eatin' with my fingers. She never allowed that. Said it was uncivilized, and we weren't barbarians, so we always had to use a knife and fork. I think the food tastes even better, eatin' it like this."

"It probably does," Jeb agreed. "I've always thought food tastes better out in the wide open. Eat up so we can hit the trail."

The meal was finished, the plates, mugs, frying pan and coffee pot washed out in the spring and tucked back into Jeb's saddlebags. When they remounted and started off once again, Jeb pointed out a disturbed patch in the wall of vegetation lining the sides of the trail.

"Nate, remember what I said about a Ranger needs to observe everything? See those broken branches over there?"

"Yeah."

"Take a closer look. Tell me what you see."

Nate studied the opening carefully.

"There's some long black hairs hangin' from one of the branches. Also a small scrap of red cloth."

"You've got good eyes," Jake praised. "Those hairs are from a bay or black horse's tail, or mebbe a blue roan or dark gray, even a buckskin or dun. And the cloth was torn from a shirt. A man rode outta the brush here. You can tell he came out rather'n went in by the direction the branches are bent and broken."

"A rustler?"

"Possibly, but more likely a brush-poppin' cowboy chasin' a stray longhorn or some mavericks."

"Brush-poppin'?"

"It's an expression that comes from the sound a horse makes when it crashes through the scrub chasin' a cow. Kind of a poppin' sound. Anyway, it don't make no nevermind to us. Those broken branches are already wilted, so whoever was here is long gone."

Jeb spurred Dudley into motion.

***

Jeb and Nate rode until just before sunset, when Jeb called a halt alongside a shallow creek which fed into the San Saba.

"We'll stop here for the night," he said. "Plenty of grass and water for the horses, and sundown's not that far off. It'll be dark soon."

They dismounted.

"Now I'm gonna show you how to care for your horse the right way," Jeb said. "Get your brushes and the hoof pick out of your saddlebags. And remember, you always care for your horse before yourself. Always."

"Okay, Jeb."

Nate dug the currycomb, dandy brush, and hoof pick out of his saddlebags.

"Put those down for now and unsaddle your horse."

"Okay."

Nate took the saddle and blanket from Big Red's back.

"You stand your saddle on end, like so, so it'll dry out underneath," Jeb explained. "Hang the blanket from a branch of that oak. If there wasn't a tree handy, you'd spread it on the ground, damp side up, to dry. A wet saddle blanket'll irritate your horse's back and make him unfit to ride. And you want the saddle to dry out so the leather and linin' won't mold or rot. Besides, you'll be usin' it for your pillow. Then, take his bridle off."

Nate did as told, while Jeb stripped the gear from Dudley.

"Good. Now, take your currycomb and get as much sweat and dirt out of your horse's hide as possible. Use it in a circular motion, but not on his legs. Then take the brush and brush him out, includin' his legs. Long smooth strokes with that. Get him as dry as you can."

Jeb groomed his own horse and watched with approval while Nate rubbed down Red.

"You did just fine," he said. "Now I'm gonna show you how to clean out his feet. I don't need to tell you how important that is."

"I reckon not."

"Good. Stand alongside his leg, like so. Stay in close so even if he does kick you it won't hurt all that much."

Nate stood alongside Red's left fore hoof, holding the pick.

"Pick up his foot. If he won't lift it, pinch the back of his leg, just above the fetlock. There's nerves and tendons there. That'll make him pick it up."

Nate bent down to pick up Red's foot. The horse gave it to him readily.

"Good. You're doin' fine, Nate. Now dig all the dirt out of his hoof. Work from the heel to toe. Make certain you get any grit or pebbles out of the grooves between the frog and sole."

"The frog?" Nate said. "You mean Red's hoof is gonna croak?"

"That's as bad of one of *my* jokes. No, the frog is the wedge of soft tissue that runs down the middle of the hoof, from the heel almost to the toe. It absorbs a lot of pressure, so you don't want it bruised."

Nate finished cleaning out Red's feet, then, while Jeb started a fire, led the horses to the creek for a drink, then picketed them to graze. He and Jeb ate a quick supper of bacon, beans, and biscuits, then rolled in their blankets. Jeb was quickly asleep, snoring softly, while Nate, head pillowed on his saddle, lay on his back, gazing up at the myriad stars pinpricking the inky black of the night sky.

"Sure wish you were here with me, Jonathan," he whispered. "You'd really love it out here. And I know you'd've been a great Texas Ranger. I miss you somethin' fierce, big brother, even more than I miss mom and dad. Well, there's nothin' I can do except try and be a man to make all of you proud. And I'll do my best to make that happen, I promise you."

With that vow in his heart and a prayer on his lips, Nate drifted off to sleep.

***

Sometime later, Nate was awakened by a soft sound, the sound of Big Red nickering uneasily. He started to sit up.

"Shh, Nate. Don't make a move," Jeb hissed. He slid his Colt from under his blankets.

Big Red nickered again, more loudly, as did Dudley. Both horses were standing stock-still, their ears pricked sharply forward as they gazed into the dark. A figure emerged from the brush, edging toward the horses.

"Hold it right there, mister!" Jeb's voice cut through the night like the crack of a whip. The intruder turned, and smoke and flame blasted from his gun. His bullet thudded into the dirt between Jeb and Nate. Jeb's gun blazed in return, and the man screamed, staggered for a few feet, then pitched to his face.

"Stay still a few minutes, Nate, in case he had a pardner," Jeb ordered. "You all right?"

"Yeah, I'm okay. That bullet came close, but I'm fine."

"Good. Keep down until I say so."

They waited several minutes, until Jeb was fairly certain the man had been alone.

"All right. Let's check on that hombre, but be careful," Jeb said. "And keep your gun handy."

Nate tossed off his blankets and stood up, his Smith and Wesson in his hand. He hadn't even realized he'd picked up the gun. He and Jeb headed over to the downed man.

"Looks like he's done for," Jeb said. A large hole in the man's shirt, surrounded by blood, showed where Jeb's bullet had exited his back. Jeb rolled him onto his back. The man's eyes were wide open in the unblinking stare of death.

"You got him in the stomach, Jeb," Nate said. "Your bullet went clean through him. Think he was tryin' to rob us?"

"It's more likely he was after our horses." Jeb muttered a curse. "I hate killin' a man like that, but he gave me no choice. Let's see if we can get an idea who he was."

Jeb went through the man's pockets, finding nothing which would reveal his identity. Their entire contents were a few yellowbacks, some coins, a sack of Bull Durham tobacco and packet of cigarette papers, and some matches.

"Nothin' here to help," he said. "This hombre must have a horse around here somewhere. Mebbe we can find somethin' in his saddlebags."

They headed in the direction from which the would-be horse thief had come. In a thicket of scrub they found his horse, an emaciated chestnut mare, tied to a stunted juniper. There was a bandanna knotted tightly around her muzzle so she couldn't call out to their horses. Her hide was salt and sweat encrusted. Bloody spur gouges, still damp, marred her sides. When Jeb pulled the bandanna off her nose, she whickered pitifully. Jeb cursed.

"Can't tolerate a man who'd treat a horse like this. There's no call for it. Now I don't feel so bad about pluggin' him." He stroked the mare's nose. "Easy, girl. It's all right now."

"I'm sure glad he didn't get our horses," Nate said. "I can't stand the thought of Red bein' treated like that."

"You're right. I can't either," Jeb agreed. "Plus if he had gotten our horses that means you'n I'd most likely be dead right now, shot fulla lead. And some of those buzzards that were feedin' on that hog this mornin' would be chowin' down on us instead."

Jeb went through the saddlebags and gear, again finding no clue as to the man's identity.

"Nothin' here we can use, Nate," he said. "Reckon we'll haul this hombre to camp with us. We'll be there tomorrow just before sundown. Mebbe one of the boys'll recognize him. Why don't you take care of his horse while I wrap and tie his body in some blankets? Then picket her with our broncs."

"All right."

Nate untied the mare, then he and Jeb took her back to where her rider lay dead. The horse shied at the smell of blood, but Jeb soothed her with his soft voice. He pulled the saddle off her and while Nate groomed and then picketed her to graze, Jeb wrapped the body in the dead man's blankets. Those chores done, and with it still several hours to sunrise, both lay back down to get back to sleep.

Despite the excitement and danger of the brief gunfight, Nate slept soundly, until Jeb roused him just before dawn. By the time the sun was just topping the eastern horizon, they were already back on the trail.

6

It was two hours before sunset the next day when they reached the Ranger encampment, which was situated in a hollow at a bend of the San Saba.

"There it is, Nate. Home, for the next couple of months, at least. Seems like everyone's in from the field. Look it over."

The camp consisted of a number of tents surrounding a firepit. Off to the left was a rope corral which contained the Rangers' horses, along with several pack mules. Next to that was a canvas topped-wagon, which evidently held supplies. Four men were posted as sentries on high points around the camp. Since the river ran a bit deeper here, large cottonwood and towering cypress trees provided welcome shade. One of the men was emerging from the brush, buttoning his pants, apparently having just relieved himself. Four men were playing cards in front of one of the tents. Others were mending clothes or tack, while a few were stretched out on the ground, dozing. At the river two men were on the bank washing clothes, while three more were in the water, scrubbing themselves.

"What d'ya think, Nate?"

Nate grunted and arched his back to work out a kink.

"Does this mean we won't have to do any more ridin' for a while?"

"Most likely. But it's the Rangers, so I can't make any promises."

"Then let's get down there." Nate urged his horse forward.

"Hold up a minute, pard," Jeb called after him, spurring

Dudley to keep up.

As they neared the camp, one of the sentries challenged them. He was a grizzled old man with a week's worth of gray stubble coating his jaw.

"Hold it right there. Don't make a move, or I'll put bullets right through your gizzards. State your business."

"Shorty, you know who I am. Can't you see the badge I'm wearin'? It's me, Jeb Rollins," Jeb answered.

"Don't know any such thing. And who's the young whippersnapper with you?"

"Him? He's Nate Stewart. Gonna be ridin' with us for a spell, mebbe."

"What about the hombre all wrapped up like a birthday present and tied belly-down over his horse? Who's he?"

"Horse thief. I'm hopin' mebbe someone here can tell us who he is. Cap'n Dave in camp?"

"He's around somewhere."

"Good. Now you gonna let us pass or what?"

"I reckon. Go on in."

"Thanks, Shorty."

"That hombre sure is a nasty old coot," Nate said, once they were out of earshot.

"Shorty? He's not so bad. Name's Shorty Beach. Been a Ranger a long time, since before the War, in fact. Sure, he's cantankerous, but you get in a fight and you want Shorty alongside you."

As they rode through the camp, Jeb exchanged greetings and nods with his fellow Rangers. Lieutenant Bob Berkeley came out from his tent.

"Jeb. I wondered who was ridin' in. 'Bout time you got back. But what's Nate doin' with you? I thought he was goin' back East."

"His plans changed," Jeb answered. "Where's Cap'n Dave? I need to talk to him. After that, I can explain things to you."

"He's in his tent, takin' care of paperwork. Third one down on the left. He'll be plumb glad to see you. He was worried about you."

"Good. You mind takin' this body off my hands? Hombre tried to steal our horses last night. I didn't recognize him, and he had nothin' on him with his name. I'm hopin' mebbe one of you boys know who he is. Have everyone take a look at him, then we'll plant him."

"Bob, did you find the men who murdered my family?" Nate asked.

"No, we didn't," Bob admitted. "They gave us the slip. We did find your father's cattle. They sold 'em to a rancher a few miles from your place. He had a bill of sale. Since your father hadn't branded his cows, we had no way to prove they were his, and not the men who stole them. Same thing happened to Sam Maverick, who owned a large ranch. He refused to brand his herd and got rustled blind. His name's now stuck to any unbranded cow, and range law says any unbranded cow belongs to the first man who brands it. They're called mavericks. We did get a good description of those men from the rancher, though. Trailed 'em a bit further, but lost their tracks in the badlands. I'm sorry, son."

"Lemme guess. The leader was a skinny dude, with pale blue eyes and real light hair. Dressed real fancy, and wore matched pearl-handled Colts. One of the others was a half-breed," Jeb said.

"That's right. How'd you know that?" Bob said.

Jeb proceeded to tell him about the confrontation in the Dusty Trail.

"Sounds like you did a fine job, Nate," Bob praised once Jeb concluded his story.

"Thanks, Bob."

"We'd better go see Cap'n Quincy now," Jeb said. "Bob. We'll talk some more later."

"All right. See you in a while." Bob took the mare's reins and led her away. Jeb and Nate rode up to the captain's tent and dismounted.

"I'll take care of you soon as I'm finished talkin' with Cap'n

73

Dave, Dudley," Jeb promised his horse. He dug a leftover biscuit out of his saddlebag and broke it in half. He gave one piece to Dudley, and the other to Nate for Red. They dropped their reins to ground-hitch the mounts.

Captain Quincy's tent flap was open to catch any vagrant breeze which might provide a bit of relief from the blistering mid-summer heat.

"Cap'n Quincy?" Jeb called. "It's Jeb Rollins."

"Been expectin' you," Quincy answered. "C'mon in, Jeb."

Jeb and Nate ducked inside the tent. Quincy was seated at a folding table, with several reports in front of him. He dipped his pen in an inkwell, then signed the last paper and set it aside.

"Welcome back, Ranger. Who's this you've got with you?"

"Cap'n, this here's Nate Stewart. I'm sure Lieutenant Bob's already told you about the attack on his ranch and the murder of his family. Nate, Captain David Quincy."

Quincy stood up to shake Nate's hand. He was tall and husky, in his late forties. Sun and wind wrinkles encircled his frosty blue eyes, and his sandy hair was tending to gray.

"Pleased to meet you, Nate."

"Same here, sir."

"Just 'Captain', or 'Captain Dave'. We're don't stand much on formality in the Rangers. Now, I was told you were headed to family back East, Nate, so why are you here instead?"

"Let me explain that, Cap'n," Jeb said. He proceeded to describe how Nate had decided to remain in Texas, and what had transpired during the confrontation and gunfight with the Stevenson gang in the Dusty Trail Saloon.

"So I thought mebbe the Rangers could use another man," Jeb concluded.

"I see," Quincy said. "Exactly how old are you, Nate?"

"He's sixteen," Jeb answered, before Nate could reply.

"Sixteen? That's a mite too young to join the Rangers. Man has to be eighteen to sign on with the outfit."

"Heck, Cap'n, Hoot Harrison's no more'n sixteen and we all know it," Jeb protested. "He claims to be eighteen, but he dang for sure ain't. And there's been Rangers as young as fourteen, even younger."

"I know that. I don't need a lesson in Ranger history," Quincy answered. "But that was back in the early days, when the Rangers were a volunteer organization."

"Look, Nate's not askin' to be put on as a full Ranger right away," Jeb answered. "He's willin' to prove himself first. All he wants is that chance. I thought mebbe he could be taken on as George's assistant, helpin' with the cookin' and camp chores, and as a general all-around helper for the men. Meantime, he can be learnin' everythin' he needs to know about Rangerin'. What d'ya say?"

Quincy looked at Nate.

"You'd really like to be a Ranger, son?"

"I believe I would, Cap'n."

"I see. Do you have any type of experience at all? How good a shot are you?"

"I don't know," Nate admitted. "I haven't really fired a gun."

"Hmm. What about close quarter fighting? Do you know how to use your fists?"

"Only had a few fistfights with my brother and my friends back in Wilmington, and those weren't much. More like shovin' matches."

"So, it's clear you wouldn't know how to use a knife, either. What about tracking?"

"Jeb's been teaching me about that on our way here."

"And he's picked up on that real quick, Cap'n," Jeb said. "I'd wager he'll be one of the best trackers in the Rangers, given a little time. He's good at readin' sign, too."

"Still, he's awfully green. It appears he isn't all that used to riding, either. Rangers spend most of their time in the saddle. You know that."

Nate was standing spraddle-legged, trying to lessen the aches in his back, butt, legs, and groin from two days of hard riding.

"Sure he is, Cap'n. I'll admit that, and so will Nate. But all of us were, at one time. And don't forget—Nate, here, saved me

from a bullet in my guts when he took on that outlaw. He never
flinched when that horse thief we brought in took a shot at us,
and his bullet barely missed Nate's head. And he never once
complained about the steady ridin'. He's a man to ride the river
with."

"I'd do my best to be a good Ranger," Nate added. "All I'm
asking is the chance to prove myself."

Quincy rubbed his jaw. He pulled his pipe from his vest
pocket, filled it with tobacco, tamped that down, and lit it. He
took a long draw on the pipe, then blew a ring of smoke toward
the tent's ceiling before answering.

"Nate, I believe I can take a chance on you. You'll have to
work hard, but if you're as good a man as Jeb claims, that's
good enough for me."

"I won't let you down, Cap'n."

"And you'll let us know when he's ready to be a full-time
Ranger, right, Cap'n?" Jeb asked. "I know that'll be some time
down the road, mebbe a year or more."

"No, you'll let me know when he's ready, Jeb. Lieutenant
Berkeley's patrol just rode in yesterday. They've had a tough
ride, so I'm giving them a week's rest before they head out again,
you with them, of course. In fact, all the men have been out for
longer than usual, so unless somethin' comes up, I'm gonna
keep everyone in camp for a few days. The men and horses are
plumb worn out, in no shape to take on a bunch of renegades or
Comanch'. Rest and a chance to lick our wounds will do
everyone some good, includin' me. In that time, I want you to
give Nate, here, as much training as possible. Before you leave, I
expect you to report that Nate is well on the way to becomin' a
Ranger. I don't expect him to be ready to go out on patrol for at
least a month, probably longer'n that, but I want him to get as
much learning as possible before you ride out with Bob again.
That'll be your job. Nate, are you ready to be sworn in as a
probationary Ranger?"

"I sure am, yessir.."

"Just 'Captain', Nate. Remember, this is the Texas Rangers,

not the United States Army," Quincy scolded. He smiled to take the sting out of his words.

"Yes sir, I mean, Cap'n. I'm sorry. Jeb told me that too. I keep forgettin'."

"That's better. Now, I'll swear you in and prepare your enlistment papers. Don't worry about your age. I'll just put down 'Birth Date Unknown'. That's bendin' the rules a bit, but the Rangers are notorious for bending rules until they almost break. Once we're finished you can care for your horse, then head for your tent. There's an extra bunk in Jim Kelly's tent, so you'll take that one. You'll be bunkin' with Jim, Dan Morton, and Hoot Harrison. I'd suggest you get some rest, mebbe clean up a bit in the river. I'll introduce you to the rest of the men at supper."

"Thanks, Cap'n. I won't let you down."

"I'm countin' on that, son."

Nate's papers were signed and he was sworn in. After accepting congratulations from Captain Quincy, he and Jeb headed for their tents.

"Jeb, I ain't sixteen, and you know it," Nate whispered. "And that horse thief's bullet didn't come all that close to me."

"Shush. Never say a word about that again. Far as anyone around here knows, you're sixteen."

"What about Bob and the others?"

"They'll keep our secret," Jeb promised. "Now let's go see if anyone knew who that horse thief was, then grab some shut-eye before supper."

***

No one recognized the horse thief, so he was buried in an unmarked grave just outside the camp, with a brief prayer said for the salvation of his soul by Captain Quincy. After caring for their horses and washing up a bit, Jeb and Nate spent the next hour catching up on some much needed sleep. They were jolted from their rest by the clanging of an iron spoon on a cast iron pot and the cook's yell.

"Come and get it before I toss it in the river for the fishes!"

"He means that too, Nate," Hoot said from his bunk. "We'd better hurry." He and the other members of Lieutenant Berkeley's patrol had been happy to see Nate, and greeted him warmly. All were pleased at his decision to stay in Texas.

Supper was the usual bacon, biscuits, and beans, along with strong black coffee. Nate was finally getting used to the bitter brew. Once everyone had their plates full and found seats on logs or sat cross-legged on the ground Captain Quincy called for silence.

"Men, as usual I want to thank the Good Lord for our supper this evening. Amen."

"Amen."

"Now, I'm sure you've all noticed there's a new young man in our midst," he continued.

"We're Rangers," Ed Jennings said. "We'd better have noticed him."

The rest of the men laughed.

"Besides, he eats so much you, can't hardly miss him in the chuck line," Dan Morton added, again to laughter. Nate blushed.

"That's enough. Men, the new man is Nate Stewart. He lost his home and family to outlaws outside San Saba a few days back. I know most of you have already heard that story. And since all of you in Bob's patrol have already met him, there's no need to introduce you men again. For the rest, Nate, our cook is George Bayfield. He's a retired Ranger who can still put up a fight when he needs to. George, Nate's gonna be your assistant while he's being trained and we decide if he'll cut it as a Ranger."

"Mebbe we'd get better chuck if we made Nate the cook and George his helper," one of the men said.

"Just try'n get a piece of apple pie tonight, Duffy," George growled.

"Apple pie? Quit tellin' your tall tales, George. You don't have any apple pie."

"Sure do. Bought some dried apples last time I got supplies, and was savin' 'em up until today. Baked up those pies in my

Dutch ovens. Nate, you'll get Duffy's piece. That'll teach him to smart mouth the cook."

"That's enough," Quincy reiterated. "Others are Shorty Beach."

"Already met the youngster, Cap'n. Seems like a nice kid."

"Thanks for your opinion, Shorty. Now shut up and let me finish. Rest of the men are Joe Duffy, Dakota Stevens, Tex Carlson, Bill Tuttle, and Hank Glynn. Finally we have Percy Leaping Buck, our scout. Andy Pratt, Tad Cooper, Phil Knight, and Ken Demarest are on sentry duty. Nate, you'll meet them later. We're one man short. Mark Thornton died in a fight over to Junction. He got the man who shot him before he died, though. Men, let's all welcome Nate to the Rangers."

The men let up a shout. Once they were done, Nate nodded.

"I appreciate that, all of you. I know I'm mighty young, and mighty green, but I'm gonna try my hardest to be the best Ranger I can."

"That's all any of us ask from you, Nate," Quincy said. "Men, while he's here, Nate's gonna help out around the camp anywhere he can. But his main job is to learn to be a Ranger. I want all of you to help with that, and none of you to take advantage of him by pilin' on work you should be doin' yourselves. You all were rookies once and had to learn, just like Nate. I expect you to make that easier for him. All right?"

"You can count on all of us, Cap'n," Bob answered.

"Good. Now finish your supper, then y'all can palaver with Nate for awhile."

***

After supper was finished some of the men retired early, while others sat around, smoking and talking or telling stories. Dakota Stevens pulled out a harmonica and began playing it softly. The camp fell silent as the men listened to him. Finally, after an hour, Jeb touched Nate's shoulder.

"Time to turn in," he said. "You've got a long day ahead. High time you learned how to shoot."

"Got a question for you, Jeb," Nate said as they walked over to their tents.

"Go ahead."

"Percy Leaping Buck. He's an Indian."

"That's right. He's a Tonkawa. If you can get him to give you some lessons in trackin', consider yourself lucky. He's one of the best there is."

"But I thought the Rangers and Indians were enemies, always at war with each other."

"Not all Indians," Jeb explained. "Sure, the Comanches, Kiowas, and Apaches hate the white man, not without reason I might add, since we're pushin' them off their lands, but other tribes don't. There were friendly Cherokees forced over here from further East, then they got pushed outta Texas too. Shame what was done to 'em. And we've always gotten along with the Tonkawas. Now, the Karankawas, that's another story. They were a real warrior society. Cannibals, too. They'd eat their enemy after they killed him. And they preyed on the Tonkawas. That's one reason the Tonks and Rangers have always been friends, because we took on the Karankawas and whipped 'em."

"I understand. Got another question."

"You're just full of 'em, ain't ya, kid? Go ahead."

"How come you wear a badge, but I ain't seen one on any of the other men?"

"Oh, some of 'em have 'em. They just don't wear 'em around camp or out on the trail unless they need to. That badge makes a nice, shiny target. Only reason mine's still pinned to my vest is I didn't bother to take it off yet. But you're right, most of the men don't. More and more are startin' to, though. They either have 'em carved from Mexican five peso coins or even make one themselves." He smiled as they reached the tents. "I guess you've got enough to think on tonight. Good night, Nate. I'll see you in the mornin'."

"'Night, Jeb." Nate ducked into his tent, sat on his bunk, pulled off his boots and gunbelt, and lay back on the mattress. Ten minutes later he was snoring.

7

Nate was awakened by George roughly shaking his shoulder.
"Huh?" he mumbled.

"Time to rise and shine, sonny," George said.

"What? It's still dark."

"False dawn's already grayin' up in the east," George said.
"That means it's time to get the fire started and breakfast
cookin'. Time to get outta that cozy bunk and get to work. Later
on, you'll gather some firewood. We go through plenty of that."

"All right, all right." Nate sat up and pulled on his boots. The
rest of his tentmates were still sleeping soundly. He followed
George to the firepit, where the fire was already blazing.

"Taters in that sack there. Knife next to that. Last of 'em
until we get to town, and who knows when that'll be. Don't need
to peel 'em, but cut 'em up, then toss 'em in that pot sittin' in
the fire. Gonna boil 'em up to go with the bacon this mornin'. I'll
show you how to mix up biscuit dough and make coffee, too.
And this is for you for helpin' out." He handed Nate a
peppermint stick. "Hid it from the rest of the men, so keep shut
about it. If they knew I took the candy from the Arbuckle's and
gave it to a rookie they'd have my hide for certain."

Arbuckle's was the favored brand of coffee in the West. Every
package contained a peppermint stick. Cowboys would fight over
who got to be the one who received the treat. Nate's eyes grew
moist as he took the candy. It brought back memories of home,
and how his ma saved out the peppermint for him. He
swallowed the lump in his throat.

"Thanks, George." Nate sat down, picked up the knife, and began cutting the potatoes. He would work at that for the next hour, then help George mix the biscuit dough and get that in the two Dutch ovens. By that time the sun was up and the men were emerging from their tents. They straggled over to get their breakfast, most of them still bleary-eyed. They mumbled their thanks when George and Nate handed them their plates. They ate mostly in silence, then when finished tossed the metal dishes and mugs in a wreck pan and drifted off to tend to their chores.

"Take all these dishes down to the river and wash 'em, Nate," George ordered. "After that's done, you can gather some firewood. Bring back a whole mess of it."

"You need more?" Nate asked. There was already a large stack of wood a few feet from the firepit.

"We go through a lot of wood," George answered. "Be grateful you've got plenty around here. If we were up in the Panhandle or out on the Staked Plain, you'd be gatherin' buffalo or cow chips for fuel."

"Buffalo or cow chips?"

"Dung. Dried manure. About the only fuel you can find out on the plains."

"Then I'm glad I'm gatherin' wood."

"I thought you might be."

Nate picked up the crate full of dishes and started for the river. Jeb met him halfway there.

"See George has you workin' hard already," he said.

"Yeah. After I wash these I've gotta get more firewood," Nate replied.

"If you have time to do that," Jeb said. "More important you learn how to shoot. Even if you're just stayin' in camp, you still need to be able to defend yourself. Soon as you're done with those dishes meet me at your tent. We'll get your pistol and rifle. We'll check on our horses, then I'll show you how to handle a gun."

"What about the firewood?"

"I'll square things with George. You're gonna learn to be a Texas Ranger, not a Lone Star dishwasher."

"All right. Thanks, Jeb."

***

After washing the dishes, Nate headed for his tent at a trot. Jeb was already waiting for him.

"Take it easy, Nate," he chided. "You'll be plumb wore out before we even start."

"At least the boy's eager to learn," Jim Kelly said from where he lay on his bunk, reading a copy of Shakespeare's *A Midsummer Night's Dream*. "Nate, he continued, "Couple more days and I'll be able to take those stitches out of your scalp. I'll bet your lookin' forward to that. I'd imagine they've been pullin', and are plenty itchy besides."

"They sure are, Jim. Been everything I can do to keep from scratchin' my head or rippin' these bandages off," Nate answered.

"Well, soon as the stitches are out I'll give you a bar of lye soap. You'll need to go down to the river and scrub your head good. There's liable to be lice in your hair by now. Got to get rid of those. Horseflies and mosquitoes and gnats and chiggers are bad enough. You don't need lice too."

"Stop scarin' the kid, Jim," Jeb said. "Nate, get your guns."

Nate picked up his gunbelt from the bottom of his bunk and buckled it around his waist. Jeb had already punched another hole in the leather to accommodate Nate's waist, which was slimmer than Jonathan's. Nate got his Winchester from under the bunk, then he and Jeb went to the rope corral to check on their horses. When Jeb whistled sharply, Dudley lifted his head, whinnied, and pushed his way through the herd. Big Red was at his heels. They trotted up to the fence, nickering.

"How ya doin', Dud?" Jeb asked his paint. He gave the horse a kiss on the nose and a piece of biscuit. Alongside him, Nate rubbed Big Red's muzzle and also gave him some biscuit. The dead horse thief's emaciated mare wandered up to the fence, her eyes pleading.

"Here ya go, girl." Jeb gave her a piece of biscuit, which the mare eagerly took. "You're safe now."

"What *is* gonna happen to her?" Nate asked. "She seems like a nice horse. It's a dirty shame she was treated the way she was."

"We'll fatten her up and one of the men will take her. Bein' a Ranger's horse is almost as dangerous as bein' a Ranger," Jeb said. "Lotta times a man'll shoot at the horse, rather than the rider. A man on a runnin' horse is almost impossible to hit. His horse is a bigger target, and once you set a man afoot he's easier to run down...or *gun* down. And a lotta horses get crippled up chasin' outlaws. Sooner or later someone'll need to replace his horse, and she'll be ready. Meantime, speakin' of ready, let's teach you how to shoot."

Jeb led Nate over to a clearing alongside the river, a few hundred yards from camp. Several of the other Rangers tagged along to watch. When they arrived, Jeb pointed to a log he had set on a pair of stumps. He had poked holes in the log with his knife and set twigs upright in those.

"Nate, since you've hardly shot a gun before—"

"Never shot a gun before," Nate corrected. "Well other than when I shot that man after they killed my brother."

"Never before? Thought you'd done at least some shootin' to make a shot like that."

"Nope. None."

"Did you at least watch your brother practice?"

"Yeah, I did."

"Well, then, at least you should know you have to thumb back the hammer on that S & W single action, then pull the trigger."

"Yeah."

"Good. Now there's a lot to learn about accurate shootin', especially with a rifle," Jeb said. "You've got to figure in windage, bullet drop over distance, which way your target's movin', and how fast. Then you've got recoil. We're not gonna worry about all that today, since mostly we'll be concentratin' on usin' your six-gun. Main thing to remember with a six-gun is it ain't all that accurate at any sort of distance. Once you get past thirty feet or so with a six-gun, your chances of hittin' your target drop real fast. And if you're tryin' to down a man, especially one who's shootin' back at you, you aim for his chest or belly. Lotta men'll try to aim for the head, but that's a big mistake. Too easy to miss. You want to aim for the biggest target, which is the chest or belly. I've seen sharpshooters durin' the War who could pick off a man at five hundred yards by puttin' a bullet in his head, but most men can't shoot that good, and they don't have weapons that accurate. Plus, those sharpshooters' targets were generally never movin'."

"Sounds like this might be tough," Nate said.

"It could be. But you've got a good eye, and with a lotta practice you should get the hang of it. That's why we're gonna start off with your six-gun, workin' on hittin' a stationary target. Once you've got that down, then we can move on to hittin' a movin' target, shootin' on the run, firin' from a prone position, droppin' to your belly then rollin' and firin', and even shootin' from the back of a runnin' horse, which is dang nigh impossible to do accurately. You're not gonna worry about any of that right now, just the job at hand. You've got your gun loaded, right?"

"Yeah, did that last night."

"You have a bullet in the chamber under the hammer?"

Many men left the chamber under the hammer empty for safety, only putting a sixth bullet in their gun when certain they would be using it.

"Yeah, I do."

"Good. Now take the gun out of your holster and aim it, slow and easy. Don't worry about speed right now. That'll come later, when we work on your fast draw. Accuracy is far more important than speed, so that's what I want from you. In a gunfight, it's usually the man who takes an extra second to make sure of his target who's the survivor. And never fan the hammer. That's the fastest way to get yourself killed, when the guy shootin' back takes careful aim while you're blastin' away wildly and puts a bullet through your guts. Now, aim your gun, and try to hit as many of those twigs as you can."

"All right." Nate braced himself, steadied his hand, and aimed. He fired off six shots in succession. One of them just clipped the top of a twig, the others either disappearing into the woods or burying themselves in the log. Nate muttered to himself.

"That's okay, Nate," Jeb reassured him. "For your first time shootin', it wasn't all that bad. At least you didn't plug yourself."

"That's not funny, Jeb."

"It wasn't meant to be. I saw a rookie Ranger do that. Never got his gun out of the holster and plugged himself in the leg. Needless to say, he wasn't a Ranger after that day. Main thing you're doin' wrong is, you're thumbin' back the hammer too hard, rather'n usin' a smooth motion. And you're jerkin' the trigger. You want to squeeze it, not jerk it. So remember, ease back the hammer and squeeze the trigger. Ease and squeeze. You got that?"

"Ease and squeeze. I got it."

"Good. Now, reload and try again."

Nate pushed the empty shells out of his gun and reloaded. He slid the pistol back in its holster, then lifted it cleanly, aimed, and triggered all six rounds. Three twigs disappeared into splinters.

"That's much better, Nate," Jake praised. "You'll get the hang of this real fast."

"I didn't even do that good the first time I shot a gun," Bill Tuttle said, coming up behind them. "I have a feelin' you're gonna be quite a marksman, kid. I know I wouldn't want to face you over the barrel of a six-gun, that's for certain."

"Thanks, Bill."

"Reload and try again, Nate," Jake ordered.

"What about all the bullets I'm wastin'?"

"Don't worry about 'em. Like Cap'n Dave told you, Ranger pay ain't all that much, only thirty a month and found, and we've got to provide most of our supplies, includin' our guns and horses, but the State of Texas does supply all the ammunition we need. It's more important to make sure you're a good shooter than worryin' about wastin' lead practicin'. We've got all day, and we're not gonna stop until you hit all six of those targets ten times in a row. So, reload and try again."

***

Nate spent almost the entire day practicing his shooting, not even stopping at noon for dinner. Before he was finished, his shooting at a stationary target was so accurate Jeb moved him on to firing at targets tossed in the air, then shooting while running, then even dropping to his belly, rolling, aiming and firing. More often than not, Nate hit his target. By late afternoon, Nate was sweat-streaked, his face and hands stained with powdersmoke. His right arm ached, his thumb was throbbing and blistered from constantly thumbing back his gun's hammer, and his trigger finger was almost numb from pulling the trigger over and over. He was exhausted, but happy. He wasn't the natural gunman his brother Jonathan had been, but it seemed he would be more than competent with a six-gun.

"You did just fine, Nate," Jeb praised him as they headed back to camp. "Just keep practicin' every chance you get."

"Wish I could handle a gun as easy as Jonathan did," Nate answered. "And my thumb's killin' me. So's my finger."

"Very few men are naturals with a firearm like you say Jonathan was," Jeb said. "I reckon your brother was one of those few. But, with some more practice, you'll be a man any Ranger'd be glad to have sidin' him. And your thumb and trigger finger'll toughen up right quick. They'll be calloused before you know it. Let's wash up and get some chuck. George should've saved some beans for us, at least. That'll tide us over until supper."

"Sure hope he doesn't still want me to gather firewood," Nate said.

"You just let me handle ol' George," Jeb answered. "The

firewood'll still be there to be gathered tomorrow."

***

Nate didn't even bother to stay up with the rest of the men after supper that night. Exhausted after the long hours of target practice, his body aching in places he had never imagined it could ache, he went straight back to his tent as soon as he ate and tumbled into his bunk, not even bothering to pull off his boots or remove his gunbelt. He was asleep two minutes after his head hit the pillow.

8

Nate awakened the next day even before George arrived to rouse him. He sat on the edge of his bunk, yawned and stretched, scratched his belly, then picked up his shirt and shrugged into it. Before buttoning the shirt and tucking it into his denims, he pulled on his socks and picked up one of his boots. He slid his foot into the boot and felt something slithering inside. He shouted in terror, jumped up, and kicked the boot off. It sailed across the tent and hit Dan Morton's head with a thud, landing next to him on his covers.

"What the...?" Dan shouted.

"Sn... Snake! Nate yelled. He pointed to the reptile crawling out of his boot onto Dan's blanket.

With a yell and curse of his own, Dan leapt from his bunk. The blanket went flying, snake with it.

"How'd that thing get in here?"

"I dunno, Dan. It was in my boot."

"Snakes'll do that, lookin' for a warm place to hide, but they won't generally do that in weather this hot. And they hunt durin' the night. Why would that varmint want to crawl in your boot?"

"I think I know the answer," Jim Kelly said, from under his blankets. He pointed at Hoot Harrison, who was still in bed, shaking with mirth.

"Hoot?" Dan said.

"What?"

"You put that snake in Nate's boot, didn't you?"

"Who, me?" Hoot turned to face the others, his eyes wide

with innocence. "Why would I do that to ol' Nate here? We're buddies, pardners. Besides, it was just a little ol' garter snake. Couldn't hurt anybody, 'cept mebbe a mouse."

"I'll kill you, Hoot," Nate growled.

"Simmer down, Nate," Jim ordered. "It was just a prank. All rookies get pranks pulled on 'em. But it's also a good lesson. Snakes and scorpions like to crawl into a man's boots at night. The inside of a boot is warm and dark, a perfect hidin' place for those critters. Always shake out your boot before stickin' your foot in it. That'll save you from a nasty bite. At least this mornin' there was no real harm done."

"Except scarin' me out of ten years of my life," Nate retorted.

"Same here," Dan added. "And a knot on my head where Nate's boot hit it. He picked up his blanket and gently shook it. The snake fell out and shot under the bottom of the tent wall.

"Now, see what you did, you two? You scared my pet snake so bad he ran away," Hoot said. "He was more frightened than y'all were."

George poked his head in the tent.

"What's goin' on in here? Nate, you about ready?"

"Just a little excitement," Jim said. "Nothin' to worry about."

"I'll be right with you, George," Nate added. He retrieved his boot, pulled it and its mate on, buttoned his shirt and tucked it in, then jammed his Stetson on his head and headed to help prepare breakfast.

***

Later that morning Nate was in the corral along with Dakota Stevens, who acted as the company farrier. While grooming Big Red that morning, Nate had discovered his horse's right hind shoe was loose.

"I don't expect you to be a horseshoer, Nate," Dakota said as he picked up Red's foot and inspected it, "but it's not a bad idea to know how to tack a shoe back on if your horse throws one in the middle of nowhere. I always recommend a man carry a couple of extra shoes, some horseshoe nails, and a hammer in his saddlebags, just in case. Trimmin' knife, too, and small rasp, if you've got the space. Shoe pullers and tongs'd take up too much room, but you can trim a hoof with your pocket knife in an emergency."

"How about my Bowie knife?" Nate asked.

"Too big. A Bowie's meant for fightin', not much else."

Dakota checked all of Red's feet.

"Nate, his shoes are pretty worn. I'm gonna replace all four of 'em for you. Won't be able to hot shoe him like a regular blacksmith, since I've got no forge, but they'll stay on until you get to town, even if that's a month or two from now."

"I appreciate that, Dakota. How much am I gonna owe you?"

"Me? Nothin'. But you'll owe the State of Texas two bucks for the shoes. Cap'n Dave'll take it out of your pay. Now, you watch close while I get to work."

Dakota took a pair of hoof nippers and, placing one end on each side of a shoe, clipped Red's feet until all four shoes were removed.

"You've got a good horse here, Nate," he said. "Lotta horses'll try to kick a farrier to Kingdom Come. Red's standin' nice and calm. Only wish he wouldn't rest his nose on my back and doze off while I'm bent over workin' on him. His head's heavy, and those whiskers tickle."

"You want me to shave those off?"

"No! You just leave 'em be. A horse needs those whiskers. They help him feel his way if he's gettin' into a tight spot, or if there's somethin' under the grass where he's grazin'. Never trim the hair from inside his ears nor bob his tail, neither. The hair helps keep dirt and bugs outta his ears, and his tail's the only protection he's got against flies and skeeters. I hate those high-falutin' folks who bob their carriage horses' tails, thinkin' it looks pretty. Poor horse has no way to defend itself from bites and stings. Now watch. I'm gonna trim the excess from Red's hooves and frogs. You want to remove any dead tissue or excess hoof, but you don't want to trim too close. You can cripple a horse if you do."

91

Dakota took a curved-bladed knife and removed dead tissue from Dakota's frogs and trimmed the edges of his hooves.

"Now, I'm gonna rasp 'em down nice and even. You want the same length all around."

He took a large rasp and filed down the hooves.

"Now, we put the shoes on. I'll hold 'em up to Red's feet, take 'em and pound 'em with a hammer for a good fit if I have to, then nail 'em on. Watch close when I do that."

Dakota fitted the first shoe to Red's left forehoof.

"I generally start with this foot and work my way around. Most riders check their horses' feet in that order. You?"

"Yeah."

"Good. Now look close. You put the nails in these holes. Drive 'em in like so. You want 'em to come out of the wall just about here."

Dakota hammered six nails into place.

"Next you turn around, pick up his hoof so it's in front of you, then bend down the ends of the nails and file 'em smooth, along with the hoof wall."

Nate watched as Dakota finished the first hoof, then dropped Red's foot to the ground.

"You think you can handle this? If your horse throws a shoe, either you do or you'll walk. Can't chance cripplin' a good horse for life by ridin' him with one unshod hoof."

"Yeah. I think I'll be able to manage."

"Good. I'll finish up here, then you can turn Red loose."

Andy Pratt wandered up while Dakota was nailing the last shoe in place. Next to Nate and Hoot, he was the youngest Ranger in the company, nineteen years old. He was a redhead, with a smattering of freckles across his face and green eyes which always seemed to have a hint of devilment sparkling in them. He was leading his black gelding.

"Howdy, Nate. Howdy, Dakota."

"Andy," Dakota said.

"Howdy yourself Andy," Nate answered.

"Nate, I've been admirin' that sorrel of yours. Sure is a fine lookin' animal," Andy said.

"Thanks, Andy."

"*Por nada.* I'd bet he's real fast, too. Not as fast as Jeb's paint, of course. Dudley's the fastest horse in this company, mebbe even in all of Texas."

"He's also the most spoiled," Dakota muttered.

"Boy howdy, *that's* for certain," Andy agreed. "But Nate's horse, there, looks plenty fast. Only thing is, he's not as fast as my Diablo here, I'd wager."

"I dunno," Dakota said. "This here Big Red looks like a mighty fast horse."

"He's still not as fast as my Diablo," Andy insisted.

"I'd say he is," Nate answered.

"Only one way to prove it," Andy replied. "We'd have to race each other. You agreeable?"

"What about Cap'n Dave? Would it be all right with him?"

"Heck, we have horse races all the time. Gives us somethin' to do while we're hangin' around camp. The boys'll even place bets to make things a bit more interestin'. Not that anyone'd be fool enough to bet on your sorrel. Diablo'll leave him in the dust. What d'ya say, Nate?"

"You and your horse have just been challenged, Nate," Dakota said. "You gonna let him talk about your cayuse like that?"

"Me, maybe, but not my horse. When and where, Andy?"

"This afternoon, four o'clock. Course'll go around the boundaries of the camp. You can walk it out beforehand to get the feel of it. So, we're on?"

"We're on. And I ain't worried about eatin' Diablo's dust. You'll be lucky to stay close enough to Red to even see his heels."

***

At four o'clock, every Ranger was gathered to watch the race between the newcomer, Nate, on his sorrel Big Red, and Andy on his black, Diablo. Even the sentries had been allowed to leave their posts. Excitement had been building all afternoon, and wagering continued up to the last minute. Tex Carlson had been given the task of keeping tracks of the bets. Nate and Andy were at the starting line, their horses snorting and prancing. Captain Quincy called for quiet.

"Andy, Nate, you'll start when I fire my pistol. You know the course, out of camp, up the hill to the dead oak, around that, left across the top of the ridge, outside the split trunk cottonwood, then back down to the finish line here. No shortcuttin', or that man gets disqualified. Jump the start and you're disqualified. Are all bets placed, Tex?"

"All but yours, Cap'n."

"I have to maintain complete impartiality as commanding officer of this company, so I can't show favor by placing a bet on one man or the other."

"You could bet on both, Cap'n ," Phil Knight shouted, to laughter. "Couldn't lose that way."

"I couldn't *win* either, you chucklehead," Quincy retorted. He pulled his pistol from its holster and pointed it into the air.

"Andy, are you ready?"

"Ready, Cap'n."

"Nate?"

"Ready, Cap'n."

"Good. Bring your horses up to the line."

Diablo and Big Red were moved into place.

"Good. Set. Go!"

Quincy fired, and both horses broke into a dead run. Diablo was slightly ahead when they reached the base of the rise, but Red overtook him and pulled ahead slightly as they climbed the hill. When they turned to race across the top of the ridge, they were neck and neck, manes and tails flying, both riders low over their necks, slapping them with the reins and urging them on.

Shouts of encouragement rose from the Rangers.

"Go, Andy!"

"C'mon, Nate!"

"You've got him now, Nate!"

"Stay with him, Andy!"

The yells grew louder as the horses rounded the cottonwood and pounded for the finish line. Diablo had the inside when they rounded the tree and moved ahead, but Red pulled even once again. It was still anyone's race. The Rangers yelled louder, clapping and cheering as they urged the riders on.

There was a boggy stretch at the bottom of the hill, a shallow, mostly dry creek. Andy and Nate pushed their horses even harder as they neared the finish. Diablo and Big Red hit the edge of the creek, and at the same moment, planted their hooves and stopped without warning. Andy and Nate sailed over their horses' heads, landing on their backs, the wind knocked out of them. Nate ended up in a patch of prickly pear, while Andy slid through the mud and hauled up against a large clump of ocotillo. Their horses stood on the edge of the creek, snorting and blowing.

Nate and Andy were still lying where they fell, struggling for breath, when the other Rangers rushed up.

"Andy! Nate! You all right?" Captain Quincy called.

"Yeah... yeah, I think so," Andy answered. "Dumb horse."

"Neither one of those horses ain't so dumb," Ken said. "Can't blame 'em for stoppin' like that, since they weren't sure what the footin' would be when they hit that mud."

"Boy howdy, that's for certain," Tim added. "They had no idea how deep the water in that creek was, either. With the clouds and sky reflectin' in that water, it probably looked ten feet deep to your broncs. Heck, I'd have stopped short and sent you boys flyin' if I'd been Red or Diablo. That's why folks say horses have horse sense. Most of 'em know better than to get themselves into a pickle they can't get out of."

"I reckon these two don't need a lecture right about now," Captain Quincy said. He offered Nate a hand up.

"How about you, Nate? You hurt?"

"Nah. I think... everything's in one piece."

"Jim, we'd better get both these youngsters back to the camp so you can check 'em over, just to be sure," Quincy ordered.

"Ken, Tad, Tim, Tom, give Jim a hand. Bill, Hank, get their horses."

Andy and Nate were pulled to their feet. Both moaned. They walked stiffly back to the camp. When they sat down, both cried out in pain.

"Just what I expected," Jim said, laughing.

"What?" Quincy asked.

"Both these boys ended up in some cactus. Their backsides are full of needles. I'm gonna have to pull those out."

"Oh, no you ain't," Andy protested.

"Same goes for me," Nate added.

"Neither of you have a choice," Jim answered. "If I don't pull those spines out they'll only work their way in deeper, which'll hurt a lot more. And, if they fester, you'll be in real trouble. Now, drop your denims and drawers and lie on your bellies while I get my instruments."

"Cap'n?" Andy said.

"Jim's the doctor. Do what he says."

Reluctantly, their faces red, Andy and Nate did as instructed. To their chagrin, the rest of the Rangers couldn't resist poking fun at their predicament.

"You two both look like pincushions, there's so many spines stuck in your backsides," Jim said. "I guess I'll start with you first, Nate."

With tweezers and pliers, he began to remove the offending spines from Nate's bottom. Nate yelped and winced with every tug. Blood oozed when Jim removed some of the deeper spines.

"Hey, Nate, Andy. You don't mind us *needling* you a little, do you?" Lieutenant Bob asked.

"These boys got stuck, no '*butts*' about it," Joe added.

"Got a little *behind* in their work," Shorty said.

"Should've turned the other cheek... I mean, *cheeks*," Ed put in.

"Men, I'd like to propose a toast to our two flyin' comrades," Jeb said. He raised an imaginary glass. "*Bottoms up!*"

"If y'all would just shut up, we'd appreciate it," Andy

muttered. "Better still, why not just leave me'n Nate alone in our misery?"

"Not a chance," Jeb answered. "We couldn't leave our pardners all alone and without companionship when they've been hurt so bad, could we, fellers?"

"No, not a chance."

"Not at all."

"Wouldn't be fittin'."

"There you have it, boys," Jeb said. "We'll be stayin'. Only one question. Who won the race? I guess it was a tie."

"I dunno," George said. "Nate flew farther before hittin' the dirt, so I'd say he won."

"But Andy slid farther, so I'd say it was him," Hoot replied.

"No sure way to tell," Captain Quincy said. "Of course, we could have Jim count the number of cactus needles he pulls out of their backsides. Man with the most needles wins."

"I sure ain't sittin' here countin' how many spines I pull out of these two idiots," Jim said. "Their horses are smarter than they are." He paused. "And that's enough *cracks* about 'em."

"Then we have no winner. Tex, just give everyone back their money," Quincy ordered. "Jim, finish up here. Rest of you, back to work or whatever you were doin'. You men on sentry duty, back to your posts. We've left the camp unguarded long enough."

"All right, Cap'n."

Jim finished pulling the spines out of Andy and Nate, then coated their wounds with ointment.

"You can pull your pants back up now," he said. "But you won't be sittin' real easy for a couple of days, that's for certain. I'd recommend you sleep on your bellies, too. Keep from irritatin' your butts more'n necessary. G'wan, get outta here."

"Whose bright idea was this, anyway?" Andy asked, as he and Nate redressed.

"It was yours," Nate pointed out.

"Oh. Yeah. It was. Want a rematch?"

"Not a chance. Let's leave it as it was. We've both got real fast

JAMES J. GRIFFIN

horses."

"Sounds good to me. You ran a good race, Nate."

"So did you, Andy."

***

Nate had trouble sleeping that night, between the pain in his backside and assorted bruises he had from hitting the ground. Still, he did manage to fall asleep after some time. He woke up about two in the morning, got out of bed, and walked over to where Hoot lay snoring.

"Hoot." He shook Hoot's shoulders. "Hoot!"

"Huh? What you want, Nate?"

"Not me. Cap'n Quincy. Hank saw some Comanches prowlin' around. The captain wants you right now. He's gettin' up a patrol to go after 'em."

"Comanches?" Hoot jumped out of bed and grabbed his boots. He stepped into one. His foot pushed into a soft, squishy, smelly mass.

"What the..." Hoot pulled his foot out of the boot and looked with disgust at the slimy substance coating his foot. "Horse manure. Nate, you..."

"I reckon that makes us even, Hoot. No more snakes?"

"No more snakes. No more manure? Deal?"

"Deal."

9

Nate's shirt had been torn when he was thrown off Big Red during the race. Jeb showed him how to use a needle and thread.

"Can't rely on your mama out here to patch up your clothes, Nate," he said. "You should always carry a spool of thread and a needle or two in your gear."

Nate was sitting on his bunk, mending the shirt, when Jeb returned from giving Dudley leftover biscuits from breakfast.

"Nate, put that shirt aside for now," he ordered. "Time to see if you can use your fists."

"What?"

"You're gonna fight in a boxing match. It's the only way we can tell if a new man can handle a fist fight or a saloon brawl. Come with me."

Nate put down the shirt and stood up.

"You mean I'm really gonna fight someone?"

"Yep. Hoot Harrison. He's closest to you in size and age, so Cap'n Dave figures you and him'd be the most even match."

"But I like Hoot. I don't want to fight him," Nate objected. "Matter of fact, I don't want to fight anyone here."

"That doesn't matter. You have to prove yourself, Nate. You don't want to wait until you're tryin' to face down two or three drunken cowboys in a bar to find out that you don't have the stomach for a fight. We've all been in these matches. In fact, sometimes we set one up just for fun, and of course a chance to make some money by bettin' on the outcome. Sometimes, two men'll want to fight each other just for the heck of it, or out of pride. No one'll think less of you if you lose, but if you refuse to fight, you won't have any chance of bein' a Ranger. You comin' or not?"

"Yeah, I'm comin'. Might as well get it over with."

"You'll do just fine. Nothin' to worry about."

"That's easy for you to say. You ain't the one about to get his head knocked off."

"I reckon you're right."

"How long's this fight gonna last?" Nate asked, as they headed for the center of the camp.

"Hard to say. Until one of you is knocked out or quits, or the captain stops it. Only advice I can give you is do your best. This won't be as bad as a saloon fight, or even one with some renegade you're tryin' to bring in. In those, everything's fair. A man'll try to poke you in the eyes, mebbe even gouge 'em out, or throw dirt in your face to blind you. He'll scratch and claw, do anythin' he needs to win. He'll kick you in the shins, or put a knee in your belly or groin. Whatever he has to do to take the fight out of you. You understand?"

"Yeah."

"Good. This'll be a straight up fight. Punches only. It's just a way to find out if you can take a punch... and give one. Just remember one thing. That's not your pard Hoot Harrison you'll be fightin', but an hombre who's a wanted man, and who's tryin' his best to keep outta jail. Hoot'll be thinkin' the same way. I'd suggest you think back to when he put that snake in your boot and get good and mad about that. *Comprende?*"

"*Comprende?*"

"Means 'do you understand?'"

"Yeah, I understand. I'm still not happy about it, but I understand."

"Good. Just keep thinkin' about that snake."

"I will. Only problem is will Hoot keep thinkin' about the manure I filled his boot with?"

"You filled Hoot's boot with horse manure?"

"I sure did. Figured it was a good way to get even for the snake."

"Well, I'll be jiggered. Sounds like this might be a grudge match after all," Jeb said. He chuckled.

***

The rest of the men were already gathered around a sandy patch of ground in front of Captain Quincy's tent, forming a makeshift ring. Bets were quietly being made as to who would win this fight. They parted to allow Nate inside, then closed ranks. Hoot, stripped to the waist, was already in the ring, along with Captain Quincy, who would act as referee.

"Good to see you here, Nate," Quincy said. "I've had more than one man wash out by refusin' to fight. I knew you wouldn't be one of 'em. Are you ready for this?"

"I reckon I'm as ready as I'll ever be, Cap'n," Nate answered. "Just give me one minute."

He peeled off his shirt, pulled off his hat and bandanna, unbuckled his gunbelt, and handed those to Jeb.

"Now I'm ready."

"Good. Nate, as the other men already know, since they've all been through this, there are only a few rules. No biting, kicking, spitting or throwing dirt in your opponent's face. No poking or gouging at the eyes. No head-butting. However, any type of punch is allowed, and any part of your opponent's body is a fair target. There will be no rounds. The fight will continue until one of you is knocked out, one of you quits, or I stop it. Do you have any questions?"

"No, Cap'n."

"How about you, Hoot?"

"No, Cap'n."

"Good. Now, shake hands and then come out fightin'."

Nate and Hoot shook hands, then backed away, glaring at each other. They circled for a few minutes, each looking for an advantage, then Hoot feinted a punch to Nate's chin. When Nate raised his arm to block the blow, Hoot sank his left fist into Nate's belly. Nate doubled over slightly, then staggered back, gasping. Hoot aimed another punch at Nate's chin. Again, Nate raised an arm to parry the blow, and Hoot slammed another punch to his belly. Nate jackknifed and dropped to his knees, holding his middle and fighting for air. Hoot danced around him.

"You got him, Hoot!" Tim yelled. "Finish him off!"

Nate struggled to his feet and weaved toward Hoot. He got in a jab to Hoot's jaw and hit him in the ribs. Hoot countered with an uppercut to Nate's chin, this time connecting, knocking him back. He followed up with a right and a left to Nate's gut. Nate went down and curled up on his side, arms wrapped around his middle. The men hooted and hollered, sensing a quick end to the fight. Captain Quincy stood over the downed youngster.

"You want to quit, son?"

"Not... not yet," Nate gasped. He rolled onto his stomach, then pushed himself to his hands and knees.

"Get up, Nate!" Jeb shouted. "Get up, kid. You can handle him. You've just got to believe that."

"Just like in our horse race, Nate," Andy hollered. "You didn't quit then. Don't quit now. You've got a lot of fight left in you!"

Nate struggled to his feet. Captain Quincy kept the two fighters separated for a moment, then let them close again. Once more, Hoot's first punch landed smack in the center of Nate's belly. Nate's breathing was ragged now, blood dripping from his chin and trickling from the corner of his mouth.

"Protect your belly, Nate!" Jed yelled. "He knows you're not guardin' your middle. Protect that belly! Hoot hits you in the gut one more time and you're finished!"

Nate nodded at Jed. He closed in on Hoot, landing a right to his stomach, then a left to the point of his chin that staggered him. A following punch took Hoot in his left eye, swelling it shut, then he stumbled into another shot to his jaw. Nate moved in for the kill, readying a terrific right to Hoot's face. He was stopped in his tracks when Hoot ducked the blow and sank his fist wrist-deep into Nate's belly. Nate folded into a right to his chin, which snapped his head back and drove him halfway across the makeshift ring. He landed on his back, out cold. Captain Quincy grabbed Hoot's wrist and lifted his arm high.

"We have a winner! Hoot Harrison, by a knockout!"

Most of the men cheered, having placed their money on Hoot to win. Jeb picked up a bucket of water. He, Andy, and Jim walked up to Nate. Jeb dumped the water over his head. Nate spluttered.

"Huh? What?"

"Take it easy, Nate. The fight's over," Jeb said.

"I... lost, didn't I?"

"Yeah, I reckon you did," Andy said.

"But you put up one heckuva fight," Jeb added.

"Don't matter. I lost."

"Yeah, but you never quit," Jeb said. "That's what really counts. That's what we like to see in a Ranger, a man who never quits."

"And if you ever learn to keep from gettin' slugged in the gut you might actually win a fight someday," Andy said.

"Reckon... I did... let him get me there... few times."

"A few times! You might as well've had a target painted on your belly, Nate," Jeb said, with a laugh. "Once you're feelin' a bit better I'll show you how to protect your middle."

"All right. I'd appreciate that."

"You think you can stand up, Nate?" Jim asked.

"Maybe. With a little help."

"All right."

Jim pulled Nate to his feet. Jeb and Andy draped his arms around their shoulders.

"Take him to my tent, just so I can check him over. I don't think he's hurt bad, but let's make sure."

"All right."

Hoot came over, along with Captain Quincy.

"Good fight, Nate. You almost had me," Hoot said. "Next time I'd put my money on you."

"Yeah. You did a fine job, Nate," Quincy added.

"Thanks, Hoot, Thanks, Cap'n."

The other men patted Nate on the back as he was helped toward Jim's tent, congratulating him on a fight well fought.

"Couple of years and that kid'll be someone to reckon with," Shorty said.

"You just said a mouthful," Joe answered.

10

Two days after their fight, Nate and Hoot were stiff and sore from the beating each had taken, but had suffered no serious injuries. Their faces were battered and bruised, Nate's smile was kind of lopsided, but all in all they were feeling all right. They were sitting on the edge of their bunks playing cards, a pastime which Nate's mother had never allowed. Her belief was that card playing, even just for amusement, led to gambling, and all gambling was evil. She had come home one time to find Jonathan and Nate with a deck of cards. She immediately grabbed the cards, threw them in the stove, and watched them burn. She confined her sons to their rooms for three days. However, in his short time with the Rangers, Nate had come to realize gambling was a part of their way of life. Card playing, dice, or betting on fights, horse races, or just about anything else, even something as simple as which of two beetles would cross a patch of dirt first, provided welcome diversion from the dangers of a Ranger's life, or the boredom of hanging around camp, far from town, for days. And Nate also found he enjoyed playing cards. It helped him relax and clear his mind. If he wanted to fit in with the Rangers, he'd have to learn how to gamble as much as use his gun, fists, and knife.

"That's an inside straight," Hoot said as he laid down his cards. He was teaching Nate the finer points of poker. "I win again. But at least you gave me more of a run this time, Nate."

Whatever Nate started to reply was cut off by the clamor of George beating the spoon on that iron pot.

"What's that all about?" Nate asked. "We already had dinner, and it's too early for supper."

"Somethin's up, and it's gotta be trouble," Hoot answered. "Only reason for George to be soundin' the alarm this time of day is if somethin's wrong. We'd better find out what. Let's go."

He and Nate hurried to the area in front of Captain Quincy's tent, where the other Rangers were gathering. Captain Quincy was there, waiting until all the men were assembled. Alongside him was a man wearing a deputy sheriff's badge. He had a bloody bandage wrapped around his head and held the reins of an exhausted horse. Once everyone was gathered, Quincy signaled for quiet.

"Men," he said, "This is Deputy Sheriff Morgan Fredericks of McCulloch County. He's just ridden thirty miles to inform us a large gang has raided three ranches in his county. We'll be saddling up and riding after them immediately. All of us will ride except a few men left behind to guard this camp, and also be available if anyone else should happen to ride in looking for Ranger assistance. George, you'll stay behind of course, since you're supposed to be retired from active service."

George snorted.

"Try'n tell the outlaws that, Cap'n."

"I will when I see 'em. Shorty, you stay here too, since you're the most senior man. You'll be in charge."

"Right, Cap'n."

"Andy, Hoot, Tim, you stay."

Tim started to object.

"Before you say anythin', Tim, I'm leavin' you behind and takin' Tom for a reason. If we should happen to get ambushed and wiped out, at least one of you'll still be alive to go home to your ma. You *sabe*?"

"*Sabe*, Cap'n."

"Good. Nate, you'll remain in camp also. I don't think I need to remind any of you to stay alert. Shorty, you'll be stretched thin, but make sure you keep one man on watch at all times."

"Understood, Cap'n."

"Good. Deputy Fredericks will remain here until he feels well enough to return home. George, feed him and take care of his horse. The rest of you men, get your horses. We move out in ten minutes."

With years of experience in moving quickly, none of the Rangers wasted any time in roping out their mounts, saddling and bridling them, and mounting up. Eight minutes after they'd assembled, a column of men rode out of the camp.

"C'mon, Deputy, I'll show you where to get some grain for your horse," George said. "Then, I'll fill your belly. Gonna be plenty of food tonight, since I made enough for the whole company. No sense lettin' it go to waste."

"I'm obliged," Fredericks answered. He picked up his reins and followed George to the supply wagon. Shorty stared after them. He thumbed back his Stetson and scratched his head.

"Somethin' don't seem right about that deputy, boys."

"Why? You think he's up to something'? Mebbe in cahoots with the outlaws who've been plaguin' these parts?" Tim asked.

"I dunno. Just a gut feelin' I got. A hunch. Well, mebbe it's nothin'. Let's keep an eye on him, just to be certain."

"Couldn't hurt," Andy said.

"I'll take first watch," Shorty said. "Andy, you'll take second. Nate, I know you're not supposed to be on full duty yet, but seein' as we're short-handed, you'll take third. All right with you?"

"That's fine, Shorty."

"Good. Hoot, you'll take fourth, Tim the watch after him, and I'll tell George to take last, since he'll be gettin' up to start breakfast anyway."

"Even with most of the men gone?" Nate asked.

"You still wanna eat, don't you?"

"Yeah, I reckon."

"Then George'll be up to make breakfast for us. I could put two men on each watch, but I figure doin' six turns rather'n four will cut back the time each man has to stay alert, so we'll all get more sleep. Well, nothin' to do now but take it easy, once the horses are fed. Soon's the sun's down we'll start the watches."

***

Andy shook Nate's shoulders at the end of his watch.

"Nate? Nate, time to get up."

"All right, Andy. Any sign of trouble out there?"

"None at all. It's quiet as a tomb."

"Dunno if that's a good choice of words, pardner."

Andy chuckled.

"I reckon you're right."

Nate quickly dressed, buckled his gunbelt around his waist and picked up his Winchester, then headed for the spot where Shorty had been standing guard when he and Jeb rode into camp. That sentry point offered the best view of the camp and surrounding territory. Nate scanned all around, then sat down, his back against a low boulder.

Had it really been only a few days since his arrival here? he thought. *Really such a short time since his parents and brother had been murdered and his life turned upside down. Those days seemed so far away now. Already there were times when his memories of his mother, father, and Jonathan seemed hazy, like in a dream. Well, no matter what, he'd never forget them. He wouldn't allow that to happen.*

Nate had been afraid he would fall asleep during his turn as sentry. However, all his nerves were on edge. Every shadow seemed to be hiding a man, every tree seemed an outlaw waiting to sneak up on him, every rustle in the brush an Indian crawling toward him, ready to take his life. The hooting of an owl set the back of his neck prickling, the hairs standing on end. When a distant coyote howled at the setting moon, he nearly jumped out of his skin.

"Sure hope no one is out there," he whispered to himself. "I still ain't practiced with this rifle all that much. Dunno if I could hit someone usin' it or not, and I sure don't want to let 'em get close enough for my six-gun."

What seemed a short while later Nate whipped around when

someone called his name. He leveled his rifle in the direction from which the voice had come.

"Who's there?"

"It's only me, Nate. Hoot. Watch where you're pointin' that thing, will ya? I'd hate to get shot by one of my own pards."

"Sorry, Hoot. I'm a bit jumpy."

"I'll say."

"What're you doin' here already?"

"What d'ya mean, already? I'm here to take over for you. Your time's up. Go back and get some sleep."

"So soon? My watch hardly started."

Hoot laughed softly.

"Trust me, Nate, your watch is over. Go get that sleep. Any sign of trouble out here?"

"Just you, Hoot. Just you."

***

Nate went back to his bunk, but didn't really ever fall back to sleep. He dozed fitfully, but finally gave it up as a bad effort. He got up, pulled his boots back on, jammed his black Stetson on his head, buckled his gunbelt around his waist and picked up his Winchester. He left the tent, figuring he'd keep whoever was still on watch some company. An extra pair of eyes couldn't hurt. He glanced at the sky. The gray light of the false dawn was just glimmering in the eastern sky. That meant Tim was probably still on watch, but George would be taking over soon.

Nate started up the slope to the sentry post. He was almost there when he stopped short. Something was moving furtively, about a hundred yards ahead of him. No, it must be his imagination. He blinked his eyes and ran a hand across them to clear his vision. No, there was no one there. *Get hold of yourself, Nate.* He gazed at the spot again. Nothing. Wait. There was something moving silently through the brush. Not something, *someone.* Nate started to follow. The figure disappeared, then reappeared. Something flashed in the dim starlight, followed by a thud and a groan. A lantern flashed to life.

"Ambush!" The words escaped Nate's lips. He pointed the rifle into the air and fired three times, then lowered it and aimed at the lantern. He levered the chamber and pulled the trigger. His bullet struck the lantern. It shattered, splashing hot coal oil over the man holding it. He let loose a string of curses. Nate recognized the voice.

"The deputy! Shorty was right. Tim!"

There was no response.

"Tim!" Nate called again. Once again, no response. Then Nate had no time for further thought, for a group of masked horsemen thundered down the rise.

"Ambush!" Nate shouted at the top of his lungs. "Rangers! Ambush!"

He fired several shots, slowing the raiders' advance, then scrambled back to the camp, reaching it just before they regrouped.

Shorty grabbed him as he ran past Captain Quincy's tent. George, Andy, and Hoot were with him, rifles at the ready.

"Nate. What in the blue blazes is goin' on?"

"It's an ambush. Nate gasped for breath. "Couldn't sleep, so I thought I'd keep Tim company. Saw someone slinkin' through the scrub. It was that deputy from McCulloch County. I think he killed Tim. He lit a lantern. I shot at it, and hit it, and he cussed a blue streak. I recognized his voice. Then a whole bunch of horsemen busted out of the brush. I think I slowed 'em down some."

"How many of 'em?"

"Couldn't tell. Ten at least."

"And here they come," Hoot said. The raiders were galloping down toward the camp at top speed. "Take cover!"

Nate dove behind the firepit, Andy and Hoot behind one of the logs used as benches. George dropped flat on the ground next to the captain's tent. Shorty went to one knee, aiming and firing at the oncoming riders.

Gunfire ripped through the predawn darkness. Two men fell from their saddles with Ranger bullets in their chests. The rest of the raiders turned and retreated.

"Guess that showed 'em!" Nate shouted.

"They won't give up that easy," Shorty said. "And we sure can't hold 'em off sittin' here like this. Scatter and take cover."

"Mebbe Cap'n Dave also figured somethin' was wrong about that deputy and is on the way back with the rest of the boys," Hoot said.

"We can't count on that," Shorty answered. "I bet this whole scheme was planned to get the cap'n and most of the men out of here. In fact, I'd bet my sombrero they rode right into an ambush too. Now, scatter and take cover like I ordered. Make every shot count. Here they come again."

He fell prone, leveling and firing his rifle as fast as he could. Another raider went down.

Andy jumped up and ran to join Nate behind the rock-ringed firepit, shooting as he ran. One of his shots hit a horseman. The man screamed and slumped over his horse's neck, grabbed its mane in a futile effort to hang on, then slid to the ground. He rolled several times and lay still.

Andy had almost reached cover when a shot blasted. He grunted, stumbled, and fell.

"Andy!" Nate shouted.

"I'm hit!"

"I'm comin' for you. Don't try'n get up."

"Don't. Don't, Nate. They'll get you too, if you try."

"I'm not gonna leave you there, Andy. Hang on."

Nate crawled to the edge of the pit. Andy was lying just beyond his reach, face down.

"Gimme your hand, Andy!"

"Can't. Can't."

"You gotta."

Nate reached as far as he could. He lunged and grasped Andy's outstretched hand.

"Hold on, Andy." He dragged the wounded young Ranger behind the pit and rolled him onto his back.

"How bad you hit, Andy?"

111

"Bad. It's bad, Nate. Real bad."

"Where'd they get you?"

"My... my belly. Down low. Bullet's in... my guts... They're all... tore up."

"You just hang in there," Nate urged. "Don't give up, pard. Jim'll be back and he'll fix you up. You'll see."

"Sure... sure... Nate."

The remaining horsemen raced into the camp yet again. One of them was a ghost-like figure was on a white horse. Hoot rose up and fired at him, emptying his rifle. The man grunted and twisted in his saddle, but uprighted himself and rode on to where Nate knelt behind the firepit. He pulled his horse to a halt and stared in disbelief.

"You!" he shouted. "The kid from the ranch back outside San Saba. I thought we killed all of you. Well, no matter. You're a dead man now."

"You're the leader of the bunch that murdered my folks," Nate yelled back. "I recognize that white horse. You made a big mistake leavin' me alive, mister."

He dropped his rifle and grabbed for the Colt on his hip. He and the ghostly rider fired at the same moment. Dust puffed from the rider's shirt, just above his belt buckle. A bullet ripped through Nate's right arm, halfway between elbow and shoulder. Nate dropped his gun and grabbed his arm. The rider fired again. His bullet slammed into Nate's left breast, spinning him around to pitch face first in the dirt. The rider looked down at Nate, threw back his head, and laughed. A bullet from George's rifle took the hat from his head. He whirled his horse, pressed his hand to his middle and hunched over, then galloped away, three of his men following. The rest lay dead, fallen to the accurate shooting of the Rangers.

11

A bedraggled column of Rangers rode back into camp late the next morning. Of the fourteen men who had ridden out, ten returned alive, six of them wounded. The other four were tied belly-down over their saddles.

"Cap'n! Cap'n Dave! Over here!" Shorty called. He had moved his men to the bank of the San Saba, underneath the cool shade of the cottonwoods. Tim Tomlinson's body was with them, covered by a blanket. The eight outlaws who had been shot down by the Rangers lay where they had fallen, flies feeding on the corpses.

"Hold up, men," Quincy ordered. "Jeb, Tom, Jim, come with me. Bob, take the rest of the men and take care of our dead."

"All right, Dave," Bob said, his voice heavy with weariness.

Quincy and the three men headed for the river and dismounted.

Shorty and George stood up to meet them. Hoot was with Nate and Andy, who were stretched out side by side on the riverbank. A blood-soaked cloth lay across Andy's middle, a bandage was wrapped around Nate's arm. His shirt was open, and another bandage covered the left side of his chest, bound in place with strips of cloth.

"Shorty, what happened?" Quincy asked as he and the others dismounted. Jim headed for the wounded men. Tom let out a cry when he realized the body was that of his twin brother, Tim. He knelt at Tim's side, burying his face in his hands and sobbing.

"Raiders hit the camp yesterday mornin', just before dawn. That deputy was part of the outfit. Lucky for us Nate couldn't sleep, or they would have wiped us clean out. He saw the deputy sneakin' up on Tim and raised a ruckus to warn us. He was too late to save Tim, though. Deputy put a knife in him. But Tim did manage to finish that turncoat Fredericks off before he died. Even with Fredericks's knife stuck in his chest, Tim was still able somehow to put a bullet right through his lyin' mouth."

"How bad are the wounded?"

"Nate'll be all right. Took a bullet in his right arm, but it went clean through. Didn't hit any bone, far as I can tell. He took another one square in the chest, but all he got from that was a bad bruise and a break in the skin. He was real lucky. The bullet that hit his chest struck at an angle, not straight on. And it seems he still had the packet with his stage and train tickets back to Delaware in his shirt pocket. They were just thick enough to stop the slug before it could do any real damage. Bullet's still stuck in 'em. I reckon the boy'll want to keep 'em for a souvenir."

"What about Andy?"

Shorty shook his head.

"He ain't gonna make it. He's gut-shot. Dunno how he's hung on this long. He did down at least two of those drygulchers. Reckon mebbe he wanted to see you before he died. You'd best go see him right now. He ain't got much time."

"All right."

Quincy went over to Nate and Andy.

"Nate, Andy, Shorty tells me you both did a fine job holdin' off those bushwhackers," he said.

"Thanks, Cap'n," Nate answered.

"Yeah, thanks, Cap'n Dave," Andy added. "How about you and the rest of the boys?"

"We got ambushed too. Rode right into it, thanks to Fredericks. Clearly, he was working hand-in-hand with this gang."

"Anybody killed?"

"Sadly, yes. We lost Ed, Tex, Tad, and Bill. Six men were wounded too, but they'll all recover."

"That's good. That's... good."

"Take it easy, Andy. Just rest."

"Cap'n," Hoot spoke up, "The leader of those raiders was a real pale hombre, ridin' a white horse. Has to be the same bunch that murdered Nate's folks. He says it was."

"It was. I recognized his horse soon as I saw it," Nate said. "Had forgotten about it until then."

"Cap'n, I shot that ghost rider four or five times, at least," Hoot continued. "Mebbe more. Never even fazed him. He just flinched a little, then kept on ridin'."

"I got him too, Cap'n," Nate said. "Right plumb in the middle of his belly. Saw the dust fly from his shirt where my bullet hit. All he did was grunt a little, then put two slugs in me."

"You reckon that ain't no human, but a ghost, Cap'n?" Hoot asked.

"He's no ghost, I guarantee you that. He's a man, a dangerous one, and it appears he's adding members to his gang. We killed some of the ones who ambushed us, but I have to admit, we took a lickin'. He's also getting more bold, ambushing a company of Texas Rangers. That will be his downfall, gentlemen. No one—I repeat, *no one*—kills a Ranger and gets away with it."

"Get him for me and the rest of the boys, will ya, Cap'n?" Andy asked.

"You have my solemn promise on that, son."

"Good." Andy turned his head to look at Nate. "Nate, pard..."

"Yeah, Andy?"

"Remember after your fight with Hoot, when Jeb said you might as well have had a target painted on your belly?"

"Yep. Sure do."

"Guess... guess it was really me who had the target on his belly, and one of those bushwhackers hit it dead center."

Andy laughed softly, let out a sigh, and lay still.

"Andy. Andy!"

"He's gone, Nate," Quincy half-whispered.

Nate buried his face in his hands and wept.

***

"Nate, you'll be fine in a few weeks," Jim said, as he tied the youngster's arm in a sling. "You won't be able to use your gun arm for a spell, and your chest'll be sore for awhile, but all things considered, you were dang lucky, son."

"I know," Nate said. "Just wish I could've done more for Andy and Tim."

"You did everything anyone could, son. Don't trouble yourself over what happened. All of the men who died here would tell you the same thing. Every one of us Rangers knows we could catch a bullet that ends our lives just about anytime. It goes with the territory, and we all accept that. You'll come to learn that, too. Now, it's time for the buryin'. We'd best get out there. And don't worry if you start cryin' durin' the service. Ain't no shame in that. Most of the men will."

The rest of the men were already gathered around six graves dug on a high point of the riverbank, where there was a view of the San Saba and the plains rolling into the distance. Six wooden crosses with the names of the deceased were at the heads of the graves, and the blanket-wrapped bodies of the six murdered Rangers lay alongside the graves. The bodies of the ambushers would not be buried. They had been pulled into the brush for the scavengers to feed on.

"At least they'll do the buzzards and coyotes some good," Jeb had said, when the last man was dragged away.

"We're here, Cap'n," Jim said when he and Nate reached the group.

"Fine. Then we'll get started."

The men removed their hats and bowed their heads.

"Lord," Captain Quincy intoned, "Today we return to the earth the bodies of six brave men, Timothy Tomlinson, Andrew Pratt, Tad Cooper, Jordan "Tex" Carlson, Edward Jennings, and William Tuttle. They were as fine and brave as any man who rides to enforce the law, as well as being fine friends. Now, as we return their bodies to the earth, we commend their immortal souls to You. We pray, Lord, that You give them comfort, peace, and eternal rest. Amen."

"Amen."

"Lord, in the memory of these fine men, we ask Your assistance in bringing their murderers to justice. Please, hear our plea, Lord, in the name of all good, honest people, and because You, Yourself, are infinitely good and merciful. In the Good Book it is written, 'Justice is Mine, sayeth the Lord', but we're here to offer You some Ranger help in meting out that justice. Amen."

"Amen."

"Ashes to ashes, dust to dust. Take care of our pards and friends, Lord, until we ride with them again in Your green pastures. Amen."

"Amen."

Percy Leaping Buck laid an eagle feather on the bodies of the six Rangers, which were then lowered slowly and gently into the graves. As Captain Quincy tossed the first clods of dirt on each body, Nate looked to the sky and made a silent, solemn vow of his own.

"Lord, I know You say justice and vengeance are Yours. I respect that, Lord. But I ain't gonna rest until that blue-eyed devil who took my ma and pa and brother away from me is dead. Whether I do that ridin' with the Rangers or on my own is up to You and Cap'n Quincy. But I will see that pasty-faced, pale-eyed son of Satan in the ground. You can count on that, Lord. Amen."

Coming soon: **LONE STAR RANGER: A RANGER TO RECKON WITH**

About the Author

Jim Griffin became enamored of the Texas Rangers from watching the TV series, Tales of the Texas Rangers, as a youngster. He grew to be an avid student and collector of Rangers' artifacts, memorabilia and other items. His collection is now housed in the Texas Ranger Hall of Fame and Museum in Waco.

His quest for authenticity in his writing has taken him to the famous Old West towns of, Pecos, Deadwood, Cheyenne, Tombstone and numerous others. While Jim's books are fiction, he strives to keep them as accurate as possible within the realm of fiction.

A graduate of Southern Connecticut State University, Jim now divides his time between Branford, Connecticut and Keene, New Hampshire when he isn't travelling around the west.

A devoted and enthusiastic horseman, Jim bought his first horse when he was a junior in college. He has owned several American Paint horses. He is a member of the Connecticut Horse Council Volunteer Horse Patrol, an organization which assists the state park Rangers with patrolling parks and forests.

Jim's books are traditional Westerns in the best sense of the term, portraying strong heroes with good character and moral values. Highly reminiscent of the pulp westerns of yesteryear, the heroes and villains are clearly separated.

Jim was initially inspired to write at the urging of friend and author James Reasoner. After the successful publication of his first book, Trouble Rides the Texas Pacific, published in 2005, Jim was encouraged to continue his writing.

Other Painted Pony Books

DUSTER by Frank Roderus

What would it be like to have money for necessities again? Could a cattle drive be the answer? Douglas Dorword is the oldest in his family, and at fifteen, he jumps at the chance to go along with Mr. Sam Silas's men on a round-up and trail drive. Jobs aren't easy to come by in post-Civil War Texas, and the cattle drive seems like an adventure in the making—one that pays thirty cents a day. The youngest of Silas's men, he is soon christened with a new name—"Duster"—and opens a new chapter in his life. Unsure of what to expect, he befriends a young Mexican hand, Jesus, who gives him some insight into how to survive the grueling days. When they are kidnapped, the adventure of the drive turns deadly. Duster's fate hinges on the rescue he's sure will never come. Becoming a man was never so hard, but giving up is not in him. He and Jesus are determined to go down fighting. Will help come for them—or will it be seconds too late?

FLY AWAY HEART by Sarah J. McNeal
Lilith Wilding can't remember a time when she didn't love the English born Robin Pierpont, but she knows he loves another so she hides her feelings beneath a hard veneer of self-protection. Robin Pierpont dreams of flying airplanes and winning the heart of the one he loves, but when he gets involved in illegal rum running to help a friend, those dreams seem to turn into just a fantasy. When he is called upon to face his worst fear to save Lilith's life, his fate may be sealed in death.

www.paintedponybooks.com

Made in the USA
Middletown, DE
22 July 2016